Robert Co...
By HORA...

CHAPTER I

A FISHERMAN'S CABIN

"Robert, have you seen anything of your uncle?"

"No, aunt."

"I suppose he's over at the tavern as usual," said the woman despondently. "He drinks up about all he earns, and there's little enough left for us. I hope you won't follow in his steps, Robert."

"You may be sure I won't, Aunt Jane," said the boy, nodding emphatically. "I wouldn't drink a glass of rum for a hundred dollars."

"God keep you in that resolution, my dear boy! I don't want my sister's son to go to destruction as my husband is doing."

My story opens in a small fishing village on the coast of one of the New England States. Robert Coverdale, whom I have briefly introduced, is the young hero whose fortunes I propose to record.

He is a strong, well-made boy, with a frank, honest face, embrowned by exposure to the sun and wind, with bright and fearless eyes and a manly look. I am afraid his dress would not qualify him to appear to advantage in a drawing-room.

He wore a calico shirt and well-patched trousers of great antiquity and stockings and cowhide shoes sadly in need of repairs.

Some of my well-dressed boy readers, living in cities and large towns, may be disposed to turn up their noses at this ragged boy and wonder at my taste in choosing such a hero.

But Robert had manly traits, and, in spite of his poor clothes, possessed energy, talent, honesty and a resolute will, and a boy so endowed cannot be considered poor, though he does not own a dollar, which was precisely Robert's case.

Indeed, I may go further and say that never in the course of his life of fifteen years had he been able to boast the ownership of a hundred cents.

John Trafton, his uncle, was a fisherman. His small house, or cabin, was picturesquely situated on the summit of a cliff, at the foot of which rolled the ocean waves, and commanded a fine sea view.

That was perhaps its only recommendation, for it was not only small, but furnished in the plainest and scantiest style. The entire furniture of the house would not have brought twenty-five dollars at auction, yet for twenty-five years it had been the home of John and Jane Trafton and for twelve years of their nephew, Robert.

My readers will naturally ask if the fisherman had no children of his own. There was a son who, if living, would be twenty-three years old, but years before he had left home, and whether Ben Trafton was living or dead, who could tell? Nothing had been heard of him for five years.

Mrs. Trafton's affections had only Robert for their object, and to her sister's son she was warmly attached—nearly as much so as if he had been her own son.

Her husband's love of drink had gradually alienated her from him, and she leaned upon Robert, who was always ready to serve her with boyish devotion and to protect her, if need be, from the threats of her husband, made surly by drink.

Many days she would have gone to bed supperless but for Robert. He would push out to sea in his uncle's boat, catch a supply of fish, selling a part if he could or trade a portion for groceries. Indeed he did more for the support of the family than John Trafton did himself.

"It's about time for supper, Robert," said his aunt; "but I've only got a little boiled fish to offer you."

"Fish is good for the brains. Aunt Jane," said Robert, smiling.

"Well, I suppose it's no use waiting for your uncle. If he's at the tavern, he will stay there until he is full of liquor and then he will reel home. Come in and sit down to the table."

Robert entered the cabin and sat down at a side table. His aunt brought him a plate of boiled fish and a potato.

"I found just one potato in the cupboard, Robert," she said.

"Then eat it yourself, aunt. Don't give it to me."

"No, Robert; I've got a little toast for myself. There was a slice of bread too dry to eat as it was, so I toasted it and soaked it in hot water. That suits me better than the potato."

"Haven't you any tea, aunt—for yourself, I mean?" Robert added quickly. "I don't care for it, but I know you do."

"I wish I had some. Tea always goes to the right spot," said Mrs. Trafton; "but I couldn't find a single leaf."

"What a pity!" said Robert regretfully.

"Yes," sighed Mrs. Trafton; "we have to do without almost everything. It might be so different if Mr. Trafton wouldn't drink."

"Did he always drink?"

"He's drank, more or less, for ten years, but the habit seems to have grown upon him. Till five years ago two-thirds of his earnings came to me to spend for the house, but now I don't average a dollar a week."

"It's too bad, Aunt Jane!" said Robert energetically.

"So it is, but it does no good to say so. It won't mend matters."

"I wish I was a man."

"I am glad you are not, Robert."

"Why are you glad that I am a boy?" asked Robert in surprise.

"Because when you are a man you won't stay here. You will go out into the world to better yourself, and I shan't blame you. Then I shall be left alone with your uncle, and Heaven only knows how I shall get along. I shall starve very likely."

Robert pushed back his chair from the table and looked straight at his aunt.

"Do you think, Aunt Jane," he demanded indignantly, "that I will desert you and leave you to shift for yourself?"

"I said, Robert, that I shouldn't blame you if you did. There isn't much to stay here for."

"I am sorry you have such a poor opinion of me, Aunt Jane," said the boy gravely. "I am not quite so selfish as all that. I certainly should like to go out into the world, but I won't go unless I can leave you comfortable."

"I should miss you, Robert, I can't tell how much, but I don't want to tie you down here when you can do better. There isn't much for me to live for—I'm an old woman already—but better times may be in store for you."

"You are not an old woman, Aunt Jane. You are not more than fifty."

"I am just fifty, Robert, but I feel sometimes as if I were seventy."

"Do you know, Aunt Jane, I sometimes think that brighter days are coming to both of us? Sometimes, when I sit out there on the cliff and look out to sea, I almost fancy I can see a ship coming in laden with good things for us."

Mrs. Trafton smiled faintly.

"I have waited a long time for my ship to come in, Robert," she said. "I've waited year after year, but it hasn't come yet."

"It may come for all that."

"You are young and hopeful. Yours may come in some day, but I don't think mine ever will."

"Have you anything for me to do, aunt?"

"Not at present, Robert."

"Then I'll study a little."

There was an unpainted wooden shelf which Robert had made himself and on it were half a dozen books—his sole library.

From this shelf he took down a tattered arithmetic and a slate and pencil, and, going out of doors, flung himself down on the cliff and opened the arithmetic well toward the end.

"I'll try this sum in cube root," he said to himself. "I got it wrong the last time I tried."

He worked for fifteen minutes and a smile of triumph lit up his face.

"It comes right," he said. "I think I understand cube root pretty well now. It was a good idea working by myself. When I left school I had only got through fractions. That's seventy-five pages back and I understand all that I have tried since. I won't be satisfied till I have gone to the end of the very last page."

Here his aunt came to the door of the cabin and called "Robert."

"All right, aunt; I'm coming."

The boy rose to his feet and answered the summons.

CHAPTER II
ROBERT AND MRS. JONES

"Are you willing to go to the village for me, Robert?" asked his aunt.

"To be sure I am, aunt," answered the boy promptly. "I hope you don't doubt it?"

"I thought you might be tired, as you were out all the forenoon in the boat."

"That's sport, Aunt Jane. That doesn't tire me."

"It would if you were not very strong for a boy."

"Yes, I am pretty strong," said Robert complacently, extending his muscular arms. "I can row the boat when the tide is very strong. What errand have you got for me to the village, aunt?"

"I have been doing a little sewing for Mrs. Jones."

"You mean the landlord's wife?" questioned Robert.

"Yes; I don't feel very friendly toward her husband, for it's he that sells strong drink to my husband and keeps his earnings from me, but I couldn't refuse work from her when she offered it to me."

Mrs. Trafton spoke half apologetically, for it had cost her a pang to work for her enemy's family, but Robert took a practical view of the matter.

"Her money is as good as anybody's," he said. "I don't see why you shouldn't take it. She has enough of our money."

"That's true, Robert," said his aunt, her doubts removed by her young nephew's logic.

"Is the bundle ready, Aunt Jane?"

"Here it is, Robert," and the fisherman's wife handed him a small parcel, wrapped in a fragment of newspaper.

"How much is she to pay for the work?"

"I hardly know what to ask. I guess twenty-five cents will be about right."

"Very well, Aunt Jane. Any other errands?"

"If you get the money, Robert, you may stop at the store and buy a quarter of a pound of their cheapest tea. I am afraid it's extravagant in me to buy tea when there's so little coming in, but it cheers me up when I get low-spirited and helps me to bear what I have to bear."

"Of course you must have some tea, Aunt Jane," said Robert quickly. "Nobody can charge you with extravagance. Anything more?"

"You may stop at the baker's and buy a loaf of bread. Then to-morrow—please God—we'll have a good breakfast."

"All right, aunt!" and Robert began to walk rapidly toward the village, about a mile inland.

Poor woman! Her idea of a good breakfast was a cup of tea, without milk or sugar, and bread, without butter.

It had not always been so, but her husband's intemperance had changed her ideas and made her accept thankfully what once she would have disdained.

It must be said of Robert that, though he had the hearty appetite of a growing boy, he never increased his aunt's sorrow by complaining of their meager fare, but always preserved a cheerful demeanor in the midst of their privations.

I have said that the settlement, which was known as Cook's Harbor, was a fishing village, but this is not wholly correct. A mile inland was a village of fair size, which included the houses of several summer residents from the city, and these were more or less pretentious.

Several comfortable houses belonged to sea captains who had retired from active duties and anchored in the village where they first saw the light.

The cabins of the fishermen were nearer the sea, and of these there were some twenty, but they were not grouped together.

I have said that the main village was a mile away. Here was the tavern, the grocery store and the shops of the tailor and shoemaker. Here was centered the social life of Cook's Harbor. Here, unfortunately, the steps of John Trafton too often tended, for he always brought up at the tavern and seldom came home with a cent in his pocket.

Robert was no laggard, and it did not take him long to reach the village.

Just in the center stood the tavern, a rambling building of two stories, with an L, which had been added within a few years.

During the summer there were generally boarders from the city, who considered that the invigorating sea air, with its healthful influences, counterbalanced the rather primitive accommodations and homely fare with which they must perforce be content.

By hook or crook Nahum Jones—or Nick Jones as he was called—had managed to accumulate a snug competence, but much of it was gained by his profit on liquor.

He was a thrifty man, whose thrift extended to meanness, and his wife was thoroughly selfish. They had but one child—a daughter—who bade fair to be an old maid.

Though Robert had made no objection to carry the work to the tavern, he didn't enjoy his visit in anticipation.

He disliked both Mr. and Mrs. Jones, but felt that this must not interfere with his aunt's business.

He went round to a side door and knocked. The door was opened by the daughter—Selina Jones.

"Well, Robert," she said abruptly, "what's wanted?"

"Is your mother at home?"

"I suppose she is."

"Can I see her?"

"I don't know—I guess she's busy. Won't I do as well?"

"I would rather see your mother."

Upon this Selina summoned her mother, not thinking it necessary to invite our hero into the house.

3

"Oh, I see!" said Mrs. Jones as she glanced at the bundle in Robert's hand. "You've brought back the work I gave your aunt."

"Yes, ma'am."

"Let me look at it."

She took the bundle, opened it and ran her eye rapidly over it.

"It'll do," she said. "Might have been better done, but it'll answer."

She was about to close the door, as if her business with Robert was at an end, but this did not suit our hero.

"It will be twenty-five cents," he said in a business-like tone.

"Were you afraid I would forget to pay you?" asked Mrs. Jones rather sourly.

"No, ma'am, but I supposed you would like to know how much it would be."

"Very well; now I know."

If Robert had been easily abashed he would have dropped the matter there and suffered her to take her time about paying, but he knew that his aunt's intended purchasing must be made with ready money and he persisted.

"I would like the money now," he said, "for I am going to the store to buy something."

"It seems to me you are in a great hurry," said Mrs. Jones unpleasantly.

"So would you be, Mrs. Jones," said Robert bluntly, "if you were as poor as my aunt."

"Folks needn't be poor if they are smart," said the landlord's wife.

"I suppose you know where my uncle's money goes?" said Robert pointedly.

Mrs. Jones did know, and, though she had not much of a conscience, she felt the thrust and it made her uncomfortable and therefore angry. But it also gave her an idea.

"Wait a minute," she said and left Robert standing in the doorway.

When she returned, which was in a short time, her thin lips were wreathed with satisfaction.

"You can tell your aunt there won't be any money coming to her," she said.

"Why not?" demanded Robert in great surprise.

"Mr. Jones tells me that your uncle is indebted to him, and he will credit him with twenty-five cents on account."

"What does my uncle owe him for?" demanded the boy with flashing eyes.

"For drink, I suppose," said Mrs. Jones rather reluctantly.

"For drink!" repeated our hero. "Are you not satisfied with taking all my uncle's earnings, but you must get my aunt to work her fingers to the bone and then keep back her money in payment for your rum?"

"Upon my word, Robert Coverdale," said Mrs. Jones sharply, "you are very impudent! How dare you speak to me in that way?"

"How dare you treat my aunt so meanly?" retorted Robert with righteous indignation.

"I won't stand your impudence—so there! Your aunt needn't expect any more sewing to do," said the angry landlady.

"She wouldn't take any more of your work if that is the way you mean to pay her."

"I won't stand here talking with you. I'll get Mr. Jones to give you a horsewhipping—see if I don't!"

"He'd better not try it," said Robert with flashing eyes.

The door was slammed in his face, and, angry and disappointed, he walked slowly out of the tavern yard.

CHAPTER III

THE WIND BROUGHT GOOD LUCK

John Trafton was sitting out on the porch of the tavern when his nephew came out of the side gate.

"There's your nephew, Trafton," said old Ben Brandon, who, like John Trafton, frequented the barroom too much for his good. "Hasn't come here for his dram, has he?" added the old man, chuckling.

John Trafton's curiosity was excited, for he had no idea of any errand that could bring Robert to the tavern. A suspicion crossed his mind, the very thought of which kindled his indignation. His wife might have sent to request Mr. Jones not to sell him any more liquor. He did not think she would dare to do it, but she might. At any rate he determined to find out.

He hastily left the porch and followed Robert. Presently the boy heard his uncle call him and he turned round.

"What's wanted, uncle?" he inquired.

"Where have you been, Robert?"

"I called to see Mrs. Jones."

"What did you want of Mrs. Jones?"

"It was an errand for Aunt Jane."

"Will you answer my question?" said Trafton angrily. "What business has your aunt got with Mrs. Jones?"

He still thought that his wife had sent a message to Mr. Jones through the wife of the latter.

"She had been doing a little sewing for Mrs. Jones and asked me to carry the work back."

"Oh, that's it, is it?" said John Trafton, relieved. "And how much did the work come to?"

"Twenty-five cents."

"You may give me the money, Robert," said the fisherman. "You might lose it, you know."

Could Robert be blamed for regarding his uncle with contempt? His intention evidently was to appropriate his wife's scanty earnings to his own use, spending them, of course, for drink. Certainly a man must be debased who will stoop to anything so mean, and Robert felt deeply ashamed of the man he was forced to call uncle.

"I can't give you the money, uncle," said Robert coldly.

"Can't, hey? What do you mean by that, I want to know?" demanded the fisherman suspiciously.

"My aunt wanted me to buy a little tea and a loaf of bread with the money."

"What if she did? Can't I buy them just as well as you? Hand over that money, Robert Coverdale, or it will be the worse for you."

"I have no money to hand you."

"Why haven't you? You haven't had a chance to spend it yet. You needn't lie about it or I will give you a flogging!"

"I never lie," said Robert proudly. "I told you I haven't got the money and I haven't."

"Then what have you done with it—lost it, eh?"

"I have done nothing with it. Mrs. Jones wouldn't pay me."

"And why wouldn't she pay you?"

"Because she said that you were owing her husband money for drink and she would credit it on your account."

As Robert said this he looked his uncle full in the eye and his uncle flushed a little with transient shame.

"So aunt must go without her tea and bread," continued Robert.

John Trafton had the grace to be ashamed and said:

"I'll fix this with Jones. You can go to the store and get the tea and tell Sands to charge it to me."

"He won't do it," said Robert. "He's refused more than once."

"If he won't that isn't my fault. I've done all I could."

Trafton turned back and resumed his seat on the porch, where he remained till about ten o'clock. It was his usual evening resort, for he did not think it necessary to go home until it was time to go to bed.

Though Robert had no money to spend, he kept on his way slowly toward the village store. He felt mortified and angry.

"Poor Aunt Jane!" he said to himself. "It's a shame that she should have to go without her tea. He hasn't much to cheer her up. Mrs. Jones is about the meanest woman I ever saw, and I hope Aunt Jane won't do any more work for her."

It occurred to Robert to follow his uncle's direction and ask for credit at the store. But he knew very well that there would be little prospect of paying the debt, and, though a boy, he had strict notions on the subject of debt and could not bring his mind, even for his aunt's sake, to buy what he could not pay for.

When we are sad and discouraged relief often comes in some unexpected form and from an unexpected quarter. So it happened now to our young hero.

Walking before him was an elderly gentleman who had on his head a Panama straw hat with a broad brim.

He was a Boston merchant who was spending a part of the season at Cook's Harbor. As his custom was, he was indulging in an evening walk after supper.

There was a brisk east wind blowing, which suddenly increased in force, and, being no respecter of persons, whisked off Mr. Lawrence Tudor's expensive Panama and whirled it away.

Mr. Tudor looked after his hat in dismay. He was an elderly gentleman, of ample proportions, who was accustomed to walk at a slow, dignified pace and who would have found it physically uncomfortable to run, even if he could be brought to think it comported with his personal dignity.

"Bless my soul, how annoying!" exclaimed the merchant.

He looked about him helplessly, as if to consider what course it would be best to pursue under the circumstances, and as he looked he was relieved to see a boy in energetic pursuit of the lost hat.

This boy was Robert, who grasped the situation at once, and, being fleet of foot, thought it very good fun to have a race with the wind.

He had a good chase, for the wind in this case proved to be no mean competitor, but at last he succeeded and put his hand on the hat, which he carried in triumph to its owner.

"Really, my boy, I am exceedingly indebted to you," said Mr. Tudor, made happy by the recovery of his hat.

"You are quite welcome, sir," said Robert politely.

"You had a good run after it," said Mr. Tudor.

"Yes, sir; the wind is very strong."

"I don't know what I should have done without you. I am afraid I couldn't have overtaken it myself."

"I am afraid not," said Robert, smiling at the thought of a man of the merchant's figure engaging in a race for a hat.

"I could run when I was a boy like you," said Mr. Tudor pleasantly, "but there's rather too much of me now. Do you live in the village?"

"Out on the cliff, sir. My uncle is a fisherman."

"And do you ever fish?"

"Sometimes—a little, sir."

"But you don't expect to be a fisherman when you grow up?"

"Not if I can find anything better."

"A bright-looking lad like you ought to find something better. Please accept this."

He drew from his vest pocket a two-dollar bill, which he placed in Robert's hand.

"What!" exclaimed our young hero in astonishment. "All this for saving your hat? It is quite too much, sir."

Mr. Tudor smiled.

"You will no doubt be surprised," he said, "when I tell you that my hat cost me fifty dollars. It is a very fine Panama."

"Fifty dollars!" ejaculated Robert.

He had not supposed it worth two.

"So you see it is worth something to save it, and I should undoubtedly have lost it but for you."

"I am very much obliged to you, sir," said Robert. "I wouldn't accept the money if it were for myself, but it will be very acceptable to my aunt."

"I suppose your uncle does not find fishing very remunerative?"

"It isn't that, sir; but he spends nearly all of his money at the tavern, and——"

"I understand, my boy. It is a very great pity. I, too, had an uncle who was intemperate, and I can understand your position. What is your name?"

"Robert Coverdale."

"There is my business card. If you ever come to Boston, come and see me."

Robert took the card, from which he learned that his new acquaintance was Lawrence Tudor.

CHAPTER IV

ROBERT'S PURCHASES

When Robert parted from Mr. Tudor he felt as if he had unexpectedly fallen heir to a fortune. Two dollars is not a very large sum, but to Robert, nurtured amid privation, it assumed large proportions.

He began at once to consider what he could do with it, and it is to his credit that he thought rather of his aunt than himself.

He would buy a whole pound of tea, he decided, and a pound of sugar to make it more palatable. This would last a considerable time and take less than half his money. As to the disposal of the remainder, he would consider how to expend that.

In a long, low building, with brooms, brushes and a variety of nondescript articles displayed in the windows and outside, Abner Sands kept the village store.

It was a dark, gloomy place, crowded with articles for family use. The proprietor enjoyed a monopoly of the village trade, and, in spite of occasional bad debts, did a snug business and was able every year to make an addition to his store of savings in the county savings bank.

He was a cautious man, and, by being well acquainted with the circumstances and habits of every man in the village, knew whom to trust and to whom to refuse credit. John Trafton belonged to the latter class.

Mr. Sands knew, as everybody else knew, that all his money was invested in liquor and that the chance of paying a bill for articles needful for the household was very small indeed.

When, therefore, Robert entered the store he took it for granted that he meant to ask credit, and he was all ready for a refusal.

"What do you charge for your tea, Mr. Sands?" the boy asked.

"Different prices, according to quality," answered the storekeeper, not thinking it necessary to go into details.

"How much is the cheapest?"

"Fifty cents a pound."

"Do you call it a pretty good article?" continued our hero.

"Very fair; I use it in my own family," answered Abner, looking over his spectacles at his young customer.

"I guess I'll take a pound," said Robert with the air of one who had plenty of money.

"A pound?" ejaculated Abner Sands in surprise.

"Yes, sir."

A pound of tea for one in John Trafton's circumstances seemed to Mr. Sands an extraordinary order. Considering that it was probably to be charged, it seemed to the cautious trader an impudent attempt to impose upon him, and he looked sternly at our young hero.

"We don't trust," he said coldly.

"I haven't asked you to trust me, Mr. Sands," said Robert independently.

"You don't mean to say you're ready to pay for it cash down, do you?" asked Abner, his countenance expressing amazement.

"Yes, I do."

"Show me the money."

"I'll show you the money when I get my tea," said Robert, provoked at Mr. Sands' resolute incredulity. "I've told you I will pay you before I leave the store. If you don't want to sell your goods, say so!"

"Come, come! there ain't no use in gettin' angry," said the trader in a conciliatory tone. "Your trade's as good as anybody's if you've got money to pay for the goods."

"I've already told you I have, Mr. Sands."

"All right, Robert. You shall have the tea."

He weighed out the tea and then asked:

"Is there anything more?"

"Yes, sir. How do you sell your sugar?"

"Brown sugar—eight cents."

"I guess that will do. I will take a pound of brown sugar."

"Your folks don't generally buy sugar. I didn't know you used it."

"We are going to use a pound," said Robert, who did not fancy the trader's interference.

"Well, I'd jest as soon sell you a pound as anybody as long as you've got the money to pay for it."

Robert said nothing, although this remark was made in an interrogative tone, as if Mr. Sands still doubted whether our hero would be able to pay for his purchases.

There was nothing to do, therefore, but to weigh out the sugar.

The two bundles lay on the counter, but Mr. Sands watched them as a cat watches a mouse, with a vague apprehension that our hero might seize them and carry them off without payment.

But Robert was better prepared than he supposed.

From his vest pocket he drew the two-dollar bill, and, passing it across the counter, he said:

"You may take your pay out of this."

Abner Sands took the bill and stared at it as if some mystery attached to it. He scrutinized it carefully through his spectacles, as if there was a possibility that it might be bad, but it had an unmistakably genuine look.

"It seems to be good," he remarked cautiously.

"Of course it's good!" said Robert. "You don't take me for a counterfeiter, do you, Mr. Sands?"

"It's a good deal of money for you to have, Robert. Where did you get it?"

"Why do you ask that question?" asked our hero, provoked.

7

"I was a leetle surprised at your having so much money—that's all. Did your uncle give it to you?"

"I don't see what that is to you, Mr. Sands. If you don't want to sell your tea and sugar, you can keep them."

If there had been another grocery store in the village Robert would have gone thither, but it has already been said that Abner Sands had the monopoly of the village trade.

"You're kind of touchy this evenin', Robert," said Abner placidly, for he was so given to interesting himself in the affairs of his neighbors that he did not realize that his curiosity was displayed in an impertinent manner. "Of course I want to sell all I can. You've got considerable money comin' back to you. Don't you want to buy something else?"

"I guess not to-night."

"As long as you've got the cash to pay, I'm perfectly ready to sell you goods. Lemme see. Fifty-eight from two dollars leaves a dollar'n thirty-two cents."

"Forty-two," corrected Robert.

"I declare, so it does! You are a good hand at subtraction."

Robert felt that he could not truthfully return the compliment and prudently remained silent.

"There is your money," continued the trader, putting in Robert's hand a dollar bill and forty-two cents in change. "Your uncle must have been quite lucky."

He looked questioningly at our hero, but Robert did not choose to gratify his curiosity.

"Is it so very lucky to make two dollars?" he asked, and with these words he left the store.

"That's a cur'us boy!" soliloquized Mr. Sands, looking after him. "I can't get nothin' out of him. Looks as if John Trafton must have turned over a new leaf to give him so much money to buy groceries. I hope he has. It's better that I should get his money than the tavern keeper."

Mr. Sands did not have to wait long before his curiosity was partially gratified, for the very man of whom he was thinking just then entered the store.

"Has my nephew been here?" he inquired.

"Just went out."

"I thought you might be willing to let him have what little he wanted on credit. I'll see that it's paid for."

"Why, he paid for the goods himself—fifty-eight cents."

"*What!*" exclaimed the fisherman, astonished.

"He bought a pound of tea, at fifty cents, and a pound of sugar, at eight cents, and paid for 'em."

"Where'd he get the money?" asked Trafton.

"I am sure I don't know. I supposed you gave it to him. He's got more left. He paid for the articles with a two-dollar bill and he's got a dollar and forty-two cents left!"

"The young hypocrite!" ejaculated John Trafton indignantly. "All the while he had this money he was worryin' me for a quarter to buy some tea and a loaf of bread."

"Looks rather mysterious—doesn't it?" said the grocer.

"Mr. Sands," said the fisherman, "I've took care of that boy ever since he was three year old, and that's the way he treats me. He's a young viper!"

"Jes so!" said Mr. Sands, who was a politic man and seldom contradicted his neighbors.

"The rest of that money belongs to me by rights," continued the fisherman, "and he's got to give it to me. How much did you say it was?"

"A dollar and forty-two cents, John; but, seems to me, you'd better let him keep it to buy groceries with."

"I must have the money!" muttered Trafton, not heeding this advice, which was good, though selfish. "I guess I'll go home and make the boy give it to me!"

And he staggered out of the store, and, as well as he could, steered for home.

CHAPTER V
"GIVE ME THAT MONEY"

From the village store Robert went to the baker's and bought a loaf of bread for six cents, making his entire expenditures sixty-four cents.

He was now ready to go home. He walked rapidly and soon reached the humble cabin, where he found his aunt waiting for him.

She looked with surprise at the three bundles he brought in and asked:

"What have you got there, Robert?"

"First of all, here is a pound of tea," said the boy, laying it down on the kitchen table. "Here is a pound of sugar and here is a loaf of bread."

"But I didn't order all those, Robert," said his aunt.

8

"I know you didn't," answered her nephew, "but I thought you'd be able to make use of them."

"No doubt I shall, but surely you did not buy them all for twenty-five cents?"

"I should say not. Why, the tea alone cost fifty cents! Then the sugar came to eight cents and the loaf cost six cents."

"Mrs. Jones didn't pay you enough to buy all those, did she?"

"Mrs. Jones is about as mean a woman as you can find anywhere," Robert said warmly. "She didn't pay me a cent."

"Why? Didn't she like the work?"

"She said uncle owed her husband money for drink and the work would part pay up the debt."

But for the presence of the groceries, this would have had a discouraging effect upon Mrs. Trafton, but her mind was diverted by her curiosity, and she said apprehensively:

"I hope you didn't buy on credit, Robert? I never can pay so much money!"

"Mr. Sands isn't the man to sell on credit. Aunt Jane. No, I paid cash. And the best of it is," continued our hero, "I have some money left."

Here he produced and spread on the table before his aunt's astonished eyes the balance of the money.

Mrs. Trafton was startled. The possession of so much money seemed to her incomprehensible.

"I hope you came by the money honestly, Robert?"

"What have I ever done, Aunt Jane, that you should think me a thief?" asked Robert, half amused, half annoyed.

"Nothing, my dear boy; but I can't understand how you came to have so much money."

"I see I must explain, aunt. A strong wind blew it to me."

"Then somebody must have lost it. You shouldn't have spent it till you had tried to find the owner."

"I'll explain to you."

And he told her the story of the lost hat and the liberal reward he obtained for chasing and recovering it.

"Think of a straw hat costing fifty dollars, aunt!" he said wonderingly.

"It does seem strange, but I am glad it was worth so much or you wouldn't have been so well paid."

"This Mr. Tudor is a gentleman, aunt. Why, plenty of people would have given me only ten cents. I would have thought myself well paid if he had even given me that, but I couldn't have brought you home so much tea. Aunt Jane, do me a favor."

"What is it, Robert?"

"Make yourself a good strong cup of tea tonight. You'll feel ever so much better, and there's plenty of it. A pound will last a long time, won't it?"

"Oh, yes, a good while. I shall get a good deal of comfort out of that tea. But I don't know about making any to-night. If you would like some——"

"If you'll make some, I'll drink a little, Aunt Jane."

Robert said this because he feared otherwise his aunt would not make any till the next morning.

"Very well, Robert."

"Don't let uncle know I've brought so much money home," said Robert with a sudden thought.

"Why not?"

"Because I don't want him to know I have any money. If he knew, he would want me to give it to him."

"I don't think he would claim it. It was given to you."

"I'll tell you why I am sure he would."

And Robert told how his uncle demanded the scanty pittance which he supposed Mrs. Jones had paid for the sewing.

Mrs. Trafton blushed with shame for her husband's meanness.

"Drink changes a man's nature completely," she said. "The time was when John would have scorned such a thing."

"That time has gone by, aunt. For fear he will find out that I have the money, I believe I will go and hide it somewhere."

"Shall I take care of it for you, Robert?" asked Mrs. Trafton.

9

"No, Aunt Jane; he would find it out, and I don't want to get you into any trouble. I know of a good place to put it—a place where he will never find it. I will put it there till we need to use it."

"You must buy something for yourself with it. The money is yours."

Robert shook his head decidedly.

"I don't need anything—that is, I don't need anything but what I can do without. We will keep it to buy bread and tea and anything else that we need. Now, aunt, while you are steeping the tea, I will go out and dispose of the money."

Here it is necessary to explain that though John Trafton started for home when he heard from Mr. Sands about Robert's unexpected wealth, he changed his mind as he passed the tavern. He thought he must have one more drink.

He entered and preferred his request.

"Trafton," said the landlord, "don't you think you've had enough?"

"Not quite. I want one more glass and then I'll go home."

"But you are owing me several dollars. Clear off that score and then you may have as much as you will."

"I'll pay you a dollar on account to-morrow."

"Do you mean it?"

"Yes. Bob's got some money of mine—over a dollar. I'll get it to-night and bring it round tomorrow."

"Of course, Trafton, If you'll keep your credit good, I won't mind trusting you. Well, what shall it be?"

John Trafton gave his order and sat down again in the barroom. He felt so comfortable that he easily persuaded himself that there was no hurry about collecting the money in his nephew's hands. Robert was at home by this time and would have no way of spending the balance of his cash.

"It's all right," said the fisherman; "I'll wait till ten o'clock and then I'll go home."

Meanwhile Robert went out on the cliff and looked about him. He looked down upon the waves as they rolled in on the beach and he enjoyed the sight, familiar as it was, for he had a love of the grand and beautiful in nature.

"I think if I were a rich man," thought the poor fisherman's boy, "I would like to build a fine house on the cliff, with an observatory right here, where I could always see the ocean. It's something to live here, if I do have to live in a poor cabin. But I must consider where I will hide my money."

At his feet was a small tin box, which had been thrown away by somebody, and it struck Robert that this would make a good depository for his money. Fortunately the cover of the box was attached to it.

He took the money from his vest pocket and dropped it into the box. Then he covered it, and, finding a good place, he scooped out the dirt and carefully deposited the box in the hole.

He carefully covered it up, replacing the dirt, and took particular notice of the spot, so that there would be no difficulty in finding it again whenever he had occasion.

Having attended to this duty, he retraced his steps to the cabin and found that the tea had been steeped and the table was covered with a neat cloth and two cups and saucers were set upon it.

"Tea's all ready, Robert," said his aunt cheerfully. "The smell of it does me good. It's better than all the liquor in the world!"

Robert did not like tea as well as his aunt, but still he relished the warm drink, for the night was cool, and more than ever he rejoiced to see how much his aunt enjoyed what had latterly been rather a rare luxury.

About nine o'clock Robert went to bed and very soon fell asleep.

He had not been asleep long before he was conscious of being rudely shaken.

Opening his eyes, he saw his uncle with inflamed face and thickened utterance.

"What's wanted, uncle?" he asked.

"Where's that money, you young rascal? Give me the dollar and forty-two cents you're hiding from me!"

CHAPTER VI
MAN AGAINST BOY

As Robert, scarcely awake, looked into the threatening face of his uncle he felt that the crisis had come and that all his firmness and manliness were demanded.

Our hero was not disposed to rebel against just authority. He recognized that his uncle, poor as his guardianship was, had some claim to his obedience.

In any ordinary matter he would have unhesitatingly obeyed him. But, in the present instance, he felt that his aunt's comfort depended, in a measure, upon his retention of the small amount of money which he was fortunate enough to possess.

Of course he had thought of all this before he went to sleep, and he had decided, in case his uncle heard of his good luck, to keep the money at all hazards.

For a minute he remained silent, meeting calmly the angry and impatient glance of his uncle.

"Give me that money, I tell you!" demanded the fisherman with thickened utterance.

"I haven't got any money of yours, Uncle John," said Robert, now forced to say something.

"You lie, boy! You've got a dollar and forty-two cents."

"I haven't got as much as that, but I have nearly as much."

"Have you been spending any more money?"

"I bought a loaf of bread for six cents."

"Then you've got a dollar and thirty-six cents left."

"Yes, I have."

"Give it to me!"

"You want to spend it for rum, I suppose, uncle."

"Curse your impudence! What difference does it make to you what I do with it?"

Robert rose to a sitting posture, and, carried away by just indignation, he said:

"I mean to keep that money and spend it for my aunt. There ought to be no need of it. You ought to support her yourself and supply her with all she needs; but, instead of that, you selfishly spend all your money on drink and leave her to get along the best way she can!"

"You young rascal!" exclaimed his uncle, half ashamed and wholly angry. "Is that the way you repay me for keeping you out of the poorhouse?"

"I can support myself, Uncle John, and for the last two years I've done it and helped Aunt Jane besides. There isn't any danger of my going to the poorhouse. I would leave Cook's Harbor tomorrow if I thought Aunt Jane were sure of a comfortable support, but I am afraid you would let her starve."

Robert had never spoken so plainly before and his uncle was almost struck dumb by the boy's bold words. He knew they were deserved, but he was angry nevertheless and he was as firm as ever in his determination to have the money.

"Boy," he said, "you are too young to lecture a grown man like me. I know what's best to do. Where did you get the money?" he demanded with sudden curiosity. "Did you find it in any of my pockets?"

"There wouldn't be much use in searching your pockets for money. You never leave any behind."

"Where did you get it then?"

"Mr. Tudor, who boards at the hotel, gave it to me."

"That's a likely story."

"He gave it to me because I ran after his hat, which was blown off by the wind, and brought it back to him. It was a very expensive hat, so he said."

"I know; it is a Panama hat."

"That's what he called it."

"Did you have that money when I saw you coming out of the tavern yard?"

"No."

"When you got it, why didn't you come and bring it to me?"

"Because it was my own money. You had no right to claim it," said Robert firmly.

"He is right, John," said Mrs. Trafton, who had listened uneasily to the conversation, but had not yet seen an opportunity to put in a word in Robert's favor.

"Shut up, old woman!" said the fisherman roughly. "Well," said he, turning to Robert, "I've heard what you've got to say and it don't make a bit of difference. I must have the money."

"I refuse to give it to you," Robert said, pale but firm.

"Then," said John Trafton with a curse, "I'll take it."

He snatched Robert's pants from the chair on which they were lying and thrust his hand into one pocket after the other, but he found nothing.

He next searched the vest in the same manner, but the search was equally unavailing.

"You needn't search, for I haven't got the money," said Robert.

"Then where is it?"

"It is safe."

"Did he give it to you, Jane?" demanded the fisherman, turning to his wife.

"No."

"Do you know where it is?"

"No."

"Boy, where is that money?" demanded Trafton, his face flushed. "Go and get it directly!"

"I can't. It isn't in the house."

"Where is it then?"

"I hid it."

"Where did you hide it?"

"I dug a hole and put it in."

"What made you do that?"

"Because I was afraid you would get hold of it."

"You were right enough there," said John Trafton grimly, "for I will get hold of it. Get right up and find it and bring it to me."

Here Mrs. Trafton again interposed.

"How can you ask such a thing, John?" she said. "The night is as dark as a pocket. How do you expect Robert is going to find the money in the dark?"

Though John Trafton was a good deal under the influence of liquor, he was not wholly deaf to reason and he saw the force of his wife's remark.

In fact, he had himself found sorry trouble in getting home from the tavern, familiar as the path was to him, on account of the intense darkness.

"Well, I guess it'll do to-morrow morning," he said. "I must have it then, for I've promised to pay Jones a dollar on account. I said I would, and I've got to keep my promise. Do you hear that, you young rascal?"

"Yes, I hear it."

"Then mind you don't forget it. That's all I've got to say."

And the fisherman staggered into the adjoining room, and, without taking the trouble of removing his garments, threw himself on the bed and in five minutes was breathing loud in a drunken stupor.

Mrs. Trafton did not immediately go to bed. She was troubled in mind, for she foresaw that there was only a truce and not a cessation of hostilities.

In the morning her husband would renew his demand upon Robert, and, should the latter continue to refuse to comply, she was afraid there would be violence.

When her husband's heavy breathing showed that he was insensible to anything that was said, she began.

"I don't know but you'd better give up that money to your uncle," she said.

"How can you advise me to do that, aunt?" asked Robert in surprise.

"Because I'm afraid you'll make him angry if you refuse."

"I can't help it if he is angry," answered Robert. "He has no right to be. Don't you know what he said—that he wanted to pay a dollar to the tavern keeper?"

"Yes."

"Mr. Jones shall never get a cent of that money," said Robert firmly.

"But, Robert," said his aunt nervously, "your uncle may beat you."

"Then I'll keep my distance from him."

"I would rather he would have the money than that you should get hurt, Robert."

"Aunt Jane, I am going to take the risk of that. Though he is my uncle and your husband, there's one thing I can't help saying: It is a contemptibly mean thing not only to use all his own earnings for drink, but to try to get hold of what little I get for the same purpose."

"I don't deny it, Robert. I don't pretend to defend my husband. Once he was different, but drink has changed his whole nature. I never had any reason to complain before he took to drink."

"No doubt of it, aunt, but that don't alter present circumstances. I have no respect for my uncle when he acts as he has to-night. Come what may, there's one thing I am determined upon—he shan't have the money."

"You'll be prudent, Robert, for my sake?" entreated Mrs. Trafton.

"Yes, I'll be prudent. To-morrow morning I will get up early and be out of the way till after uncle is gone. There is no chance of his getting up early and going a-fishing."

The deep and noisy breathing made it probable that the fisherman would awaken at a late hour, as both Robert and his aunt knew.

She was reassured by his promise and prepared to go to bed. Soon all three inmates of the little cabin were sleeping soundly.

CHAPTER VII
THE NEXT MORNING

Robert rose at six the next morning and half an hour later took his breakfast. It consisted of fish, bread and a cup of tea, and though most of my young readers might not be satisfied with it—especially as there was no butter—Robert thought himself lucky to be so well provided for.

When his breakfast was finished he rose from the table.

"Now I'm off, Aunt Jane," he said.

"Where are you going, Robert?"

"I'll earn some money if I can. We've got a little, but it won't last long."

"It won't be very easy to find work, I am afraid."

"I shall be ready for anything that turns up, aunt. Something turned up yesterday when I didn't expect it."

"That's true."

Just then the fisherman was heard to stir in the adjoining room, and Robert, not wishing to be near when he awakened, hastily left the cabin to avoid a repetition of the scene of the previous night.

Mrs. Trafton breathed a sigh of relief when her nephew was fairly out of the way.

About an hour later her husband rose and without needing to dress—for he had thrown himself on the bed in his ordinary clothes—walked into the room where his wife was at work.

"Where's Robert?" he asked.

"He had his breakfast and went out."

"How long ago?"

"About an hour ago."

John Trafton scowled with disappointment.

"Is he round about home?"

"I don't think he is."

"Did he say where he was going?"

"He said he would try to find a job."

"Why didn't you keep him? Didn't you know I wanted to see him?"

"You didn't ask me to keep him," said Mrs. Trafton nervously.

"I see how it is," said the fisherman; "you're in league with him."

"What do you mean by that, John?"

"You know well enough what I mean. You don't want him to give me that money."

Mrs. Trafton plucked up courage enough to say: "You ought not to ask for it, John."

"Why shouldn't I ask for it?" he demanded, pounding forcibly on the table.

"Because he means to spend it for things we need and you want it to spend at the tavern."

"There you are again—always twitting me because, after exposing myself to storm and the dangers of the sea, I take a little something to warm me up and make me comfortable."

To hear John Trafton's tone one might think him a grievously injured man.

"For two years, John Trafton, you have spent three-fourths of your earnings at the tavern," said his wife quietly. "You have left me to suffer want and privation that you might indulge your appetite for drink."

"You seem to be alive still," he said with an ugly sneer. "You don't seem to have starved."

"I might have done so but for Robert. He has brought me fish and bought groceries with what little money he could earn in various ways."

"Oh, it's Robert always!" sneered Trafton. "He is an angel, is he? He's only done his duty. Haven't I given him the shelter of my roof?"

"You haven't given him much else," retorted his wife.

"I've heard enough of that; now shut up," said the fisherman roughly. "What have you got for breakfast?"

Mrs. Trafton pointed to the table, on which, while her husband had been speaking, she had placed his breakfast.

"Humph!" said he discontentedly, "that's a pretty poor breakfast!"

"It is the best I can give you," said his wife coldly.

"I don't care for tea. I'd as soon drink slops."

"What do you prefer?"

"I prefer coffee."

"I have none in the house. If you will bring me home some from the store, I will make you a cup every morning, but I don't think you would like it without milk."

"Do you think I am made of money? How do you expect me to buy coffee?"

"With the money you would otherwise spend for drink."

"Stop that, will you?" said Trafton angrily. "I'm tired of it."

13

A moment later he said in a milder tone:

"When I get that money of Robert's I will buy a pound of coffee."

Mrs. Trafton said nothing.

"Do you know where he has hidden it?" asked her husband after drinking a cup of the tea which he had so decried.

"No."

"Didn't he tell you where he was going to put it?"

"No."

"You are sure he didn't give it to you to keep?"

"I am very glad he didn't."

"Why are you glad?"

"Because you would have teased me till you got it."

"And I'll have it yet, Mrs. Trafton—do you hear that?" said the fisherman fiercely.

"Yes, I hear you."

"You may as well make up your mind that I am in earnest. What! am I to be defied by a weak woman and a half-grown boy? You don't know me, Mrs. T."

"I do know you only too well, Mr. Trafton. It was an unlucky day when I married you."

"Humph! There may be two sides to that story. Well, I'm going."

"Where are you going? Shall you go out in the boat this morning?"

"Oh, you expect me to spend all my time working for my support, do you? No, I am not going out in the boat. I am going to the village."

"To the tavern, I suppose?"

"And suppose I am going to the tavern," repeated the fisherman in a defiant tone, "have you got anything to say against it?"

"I have a great deal to say, but it won't do any good."

"That's where you are right."

John Trafton left the cabin, but he did not immediately take the road to the village.

First of all he thought he would look round a little and see if he could not discover the hiding place of the little sum which his nephew had concealed.

He walked about the cabin in various directions, examining carefully to see if anywhere the ground had been disturbed.

In one or two places he thought he detected signs of disturbance, and, bending over, scooped up the loose dirt, but, fortunately for our hero, he was on a false scent and discovered nothing.

He was not a very patient man, and the fresh disappointment—for his hopes had been raised in each case—made him still more angry.

"The young rascal!" he muttered. "He deserves to be flogged for giving me so much trouble."

From the window of the cabin Mrs. Trafton saw what her husband was about and she was very much afraid he would succeed. She could not help—painful as it was—regarding with contempt a man who would stoop to such pitiful means to obtain money to gratify his diseased appetite.

"If I thought my wife knew where this money is I'd have it out of her," muttered the fisherman with a dark look at the cabin, "but likely the boy didn't tell her. I'll have to have some dealings with him shortly. He shall learn that he cannot defy me."

John Trafton, giving up the search, took his way to the village, and, as a matter of course, started directly for the tavern.

He entered the barroom and called for a drink.

Mr. Jones did not show his usual alacrity in waiting upon him.

"Trafton," said he, "where is that dollar you promised to pay me this morning?"

"Haven't got it," answered the fisherman, rather embarrassed. "I'll bring it to-morrow morning."

"Then to-morrow morning you may call for a drink."

"You ain't going back on me, Mr. Jones?" asked John Trafton in alarm.

"You are going back on me, as I look at it. You promised to bring me a dollar and you haven't done it."

"I'll tell you how it is, Mr. Jones. My nephew, Robert, has the money, but he was gone when I woke up this morning. I shall see him to-night and give you the money."

"You needn't wait till then. I saw Robert pass here only half an hour ago. He's somewhere in the village. Find him and get the money and then I'll talk with you."

There was no appeal from this decision and Trafton, angry and sullen, left the tavern to look for Robert.

CHAPTER VIII

ROBERT BECOMES A PRISONER

One of the most tasteful houses in Cook's Harbor was occupied in summer by the family of Theodore Irving, a Boston lawyer, who liked to have his wife and children in the country, though his business required him to spend a part of the hot season in the city.

The oldest son, Herbert, was about a year younger than Robert, a lively boy, fond of manly sports and thoroughly democratic in his tastes. He had scraped acquaintance with our hero, making the first advances, for Robert was not disposed to intrude his company where he was not sure it would be acceptable.

When Robert came to the village to avoid meeting his uncle. In passing by the house of Mr. Irving he attracted the attention of Herbert, who was sitting on the edge of the piazza.

With him was another boy of about his own age, a cousin named George Randolph. He had come to Cook's Harbor to spend a fortnight with his cousin, but the latter soon found that George was very hard to entertain.

He was seldom willing to engage in any amusement selected by his cousin, but always had some plan of his own to propose. Moreover, he was proud of his social position and always looked down upon boys whose dress indicated a humbler rank than his own.

The two cousins were sitting on the piazza doing nothing. Herbert had proposed croquet, but George pronounced it too warm. He also declined ball for a similar reason.

"It seems to me you are very much afraid of the sun," said Herbert.

"I don't care to get tanned up. It looks vulgar," said George.

"I like to have a good time, even if I do get browned up," said his cousin.

"Then I don't agree with you," said George in a superior tone.

Just then Robert was seen approaching.

"There's a boy that will play with me," said Herbert, brightening up.

"What boy?"

"There—the one that is just coming along."

"That boy? Why, he isn't dressed as well as our coachman's son!"

"I can't help that; he's a nice fellow. Bob, come here; I want you."

"You surely are not going to invite that common boy into the yard?" protested George hastily.

"Why not? He has been here more than once."

By this time Robert had reached the gate.

Herbert jumped up and ran to open it.

"I am glad to see you, Robert," said Herbert cordially. "Are you in a hurry?"

"No, Herbert."

"Then come in and have a game of croquet."

"All right, but you'll easily beat me."

"Never mind; you'll learn fast. Bob, this is my cousin, George Randolph. George, this is my friend, Robert Coverdale."

George made the slightest possible inclination of the head and did not stir from where he was sitting.

"He doesn't look very social," thought Robert, greeting his friend's visitor politely.

"Here, Bob, select a mallet and ball. Shall I start first?"

"If you please. Won't your cousin play?"

"I'm very much obliged, I'm sure, for the invitation," said George, "but I'd rather not."

"George is afraid of being tanned by exposure to the sun," explained Herbert. "I hope you are not."

"I don't think the sun will make me any browner than I am already," said Robert, laughing.

"I agree with you," said George in a sneering tone.

Robert looked at him quickly, struck by his tone, and decided that he had no particular desire to become any better acquainted.

The game of croquet proceeded and Herbert was an easy victor.

"I told you I should be beaten, Herbert," said Robert.

"Of course; I am much more used to the game than you. I will give you odds of half the game. You shall start from the other stake on the return course and I will try to overtake you."

He came near succeeding, but Robert beat him by two wickets.

After three games Herbert proposed ball, and Robert, who felt more at home in this game, agreed to it.

"You'd better join us, George," said his cousin.

"No, I thank you. I have no inclination, I assure you."

"I don't see what fun there can be in sitting on the piazza."

"You forget that I have an opportunity of witnessing your friend's superior playing."

His tone made it clear to Robert that this was a sneer, but he had too much self-respect and too much regard for Herbert to take offense at it.

"You mean my awkwardness," he said. "You are quite welcome to the amusement it must afford you."

George arched his brows in surprise.

"Really this ragged boy is talking to me as if he considered me his equal," he thought. "It is Herbert's fault. He should not treat him so familiarly. I really don't care to be in such company."

"You must excuse me, Herbert," said George, rising with suitable dignity. "As you are provided with company, you can spare me. I will go into the house and read for a while."

"Very well, George."

"I hope I haven't driven your cousin away, Herbert," said Robert.

"I don't care whether you have or not, Bob," said Herbert, "I'm awfully disappointed in him. Papa invited him to visit us, thinking he would be company for me, but, instead of that, he objects to everything I propose. I find it very hard to entertain him."

"He doesn't appear to fancy me," said Robert.

"Don't mind him, Bob. He's a mean, stuck-up fellow, if he is my cousin."

"Perhaps he is not to blame. I am only a poor boy, belonging to a fisherman's family. I am afraid I am not a suitable associate for you or him," said Robert with proud humility.

"No more of that talk, Bob," said Herbert. "You're suitable for me, anyhow, and I like you twice as much as my cousin. I don't care how you are dressed, as long as you are a good fellow."

"At any rate, you are a good fellow, Herbert," said Robert warmly. "I liked you the very first day I saw you."

"And I can say the same for you. Bob. Well, never mind about George. Leave him to his book. We'll amuse ourselves better."

As Robert was playing he caught sight of his uncle on his way to the tavern. He knew, therefore, that he could return home without danger of annoyance, and he excused himself to Herbert. As it was doubtful whether he could get anything to do in the village and as the boat would not be in use, he concluded to go out and see if he could not catch a few fish for his aunt's dinner.

"Well, come and play with me again very soon, Bob," said his friend.

"I will, Herbert. Thank you for inviting me."

"Oh, I do that on my own account! I like your company."

"Thank you!"

Robert went home and spent a short time with his aunt before setting out on his fishing trip. He only meant to go out a short distance and there was plenty of time before noon.

He was just getting out the boat when, to his dismay, he heard a familiar but unwelcome voice hailing him.

"Where are you going?"

"I am going a-fishing. I thought you were not going to use the boat."

"Well, I am," said the fisherman shortly. "Are you ready to give me that money?"

"No, uncle," said Robert firmly.

"I have a right to it."

"You don't need it and aunt does," answered our hero.

"Well, never mind about that now. You can go out with me."

Considerably surprised at getting off so easily, Robert jumped into the boat with his uncle and they pushed off.

"Pull for Egg Island," said John Trafton.

Egg Island, so called from its oval shape, was situated about three miles from the cliff on which the fisherman's cabin stood and probably did not comprise more than an acre of surface. It was rocky, partly covered with bushes and quite unoccupied.

Robert was puzzled, but did not venture to ask his uncle why they were going to this island.

In due time they reached the rocky isle and the boat was rounded to shore.

"You may jump out and get me a good-sized stick," said the fisherman.

Robert obeyed, though he feared the stick was to be used on his back.

He had scarcely scrambled up the bank than he heard the sound of oars, and, looking back hastily, he saw his uncle pushing off from the island.

"I'm going to leave you here, you young rascal, till you agree to give me that money," said John Trafton triumphantly. "I'll let you know that I won't be defied by a boy."

16

Already the boat was several rods distant.

Robert sat down on a rocky ledge and tried to realize his position. He was a prisoner on Egg Island and there he must stay till his uncle chose to release him.

CHAPTER IX
ALONE ON AN ISLAND

Of course our hero's position was not to be compared with that of one left on a lonely island in the Pacific, but it was not agreeable. He was only three miles from the mainland, but there was no chance to cross this brief distance. He had no boat, and though he could swim a little, he would inevitably have been drowned had he undertaken to swim to shore.

Robert had read "Robinson Crusoe," and he naturally thought of that famous mariner on finding himself in a similar position.

He had never been on Egg Island before and he knew it only as he had seen it from the mainland or from a boat.

"That's a mean trick of Uncle John," said Robert to himself. "If I had suspected what he was after I wouldn't have got out of the boat."

Just then he saw the boat turn, the fisherman pulling for the island.

Robert felt relieved. He was not to be left on the island after all. He sat still and waited for the boat to approach.

"Well, how do you like it?" asked Trafton when he was within a few rods.

"Not very well," answered our hero.

"You wouldn't care to stay here, I suppose?"

"No."

"I will take you back into the boat if you will promise to give me that money."

It was a tempting proposal, and Robert was half inclined to yield. But, he reflected, his uncle had no claim to the money, and, if he secured it, would spend it for drink, while his aunt would lose the benefit of it. He summoned all his courage and answered:

"You have no right to the money, uncle. I can't give it to you."

"If you don't, I will row away and leave you."

"Then you will be doing a very mean thing," said Robert with spirit.

"That's my lookout. Just understand that I am in earnest. Now, what do you say?"

"I say no," answered our hero firmly.

"Then you may take the consequences," said his uncle, with a muttered curse, as he turned the head of the boat and rowed rapidly away.

Robert watched the receding boat, and for an instant he regretted his determination. But it was only for an instant.

"I have done what I thought to be right," he said, "and I don't believe I shall have cause to repent it. I must see what is best to be done."

He got up and set about exploring his small island kingdom.

It was very rocky, the only vegetation being some scant grass and some whortleberry bushes. Luckily it was the height of the berry season and there was a good supply on the bushes.

"I shan't starve just yet," he said cheerfully. "These berries will keep me alive for a day or two, if I am compelled to remain as long."

There was this advantage about the berries, that, in a measure, they satisfied his thirst as well as his hunger.

Robert did not immediately begin to gather berries, for it was yet early, and too short a time had elapsed since breakfast for him to have gained an appetite. He wandered at random over his small kingdom and from the highest portion looked out to sea.

Far away he saw several sails, but there was little chance of being rescued by any. If he were seen, it would not be supposed that he was confined a prisoner on an island so near the mainland. Still Robert did not feel that he was likely to be a prisoner for a long time.

There were other fishermen, besides his uncle, at Cook's Harbor, and by next morning, at the farthest, he would be able to attract the attention of some one of them as he cruised near the island.

But it would not be very pleasant to pass a night alone in such an exposed spot.

Not long before a sloop had been wrecked upon the southwest corner of the island, and though no lives were lost, the vessel itself had been so injured that there had been no attempt to repair or remove it.

In coasting near the island Robert had often thought he would like to examine the wreck, but he never had done so. It struck him now that he had a capital opportunity to view it at his leisure. Of leisure, unfortunately, he had too much on his hands.

There was a patch of sand at the corner where the sloop had run ashore and the frame of the vessel had imbedded in it. A portion had been swept away, but a considerable part still remained.

Robert clambered down and began to make an examination of the stranded vessel.

"I suppose it belongs to me if I choose to claim it," he said to himself. "At any rate, no one else is likely to dispute my claim. Wouldn't it be jolly if I could find a keg of gold pieces hidden somewhere about the old wreck? That would keep aunt and me for years and we wouldn't feel any anxiety about support."

This was very pleasant to think about certainly, but kegs of gold pieces are not often carried on sloops nowadays, as Robert very well knew.

The chief use the old wreck was likely to be to him was in affording materials for a raft by which he might find his way to the mainland.

Our hero made a critical survey of the wreck and tried to pull it apart. This was not easy, but finally he was enabled to detach a few planks.

"If I only had a saw, a hammer and some nails," he thought, "I could build a raft without much difficulty. But I don't see how I am going to get along without these."

For the hammer he soon found a substitute in a hard rock of moderate size. There were nails, but they were not easy to extricate from the planks. As to a saw, there was no hope of getting one or anything that would answer the purpose of one.

Robert worked hard for a couple of hours and in that time he had accomplished something. He had extricated half a dozen planks of unequal length, secured a supply of nails, more or less rusty, and thus had already provided the materials of a raft.

The grand difficulty remained—to fashion them into a raft which would convey him in safety to the shore of the mainland.

I have said that he had no saw. He had a jackknife, however, and this was of some use to him, particularly in extricating the nails. It was slow work, but he had all day before him.

When the two hours were over he began to feel hungry. It was not far from the time when he was accustomed to take dinner, and he set about satisfying his hunger.

He went from bush to bush, plucking the ripe berries and eating them. They were very good, but not quite so hearty as a plate of meat and potatoes. However, he would have had no meat if he had been able to sit down at home.

After dinner—if his repast of berries can be dignified by such a name—Robert sat down to rest a while before resuming his labors on the raft.

He finally lay down with his head in the shadow of an unusually large bush, and, before he was fully aware of the danger, he had fallen asleep. When he awoke he saw by the position of the sun that it must be about the middle of the afternoon.

He jumped up hastily, and, first of all, took a hasty glance around to see if he could anywhere descry a boat. But none was to be seen.

"I must set about making my raft," he decided. "It is getting late and I don't know how long it may take me."

It proved to be slow and rather difficult work. Robert was pounding away with his stone hammer when, to his great joy, he descried a boat rounding the corner of the island.

It was rowed by a single boy. When he came near Robert recognized him as George Randolph—the cousin of his friend Herbert.

It happened that George was very fond of rowing and had a boat of his own, which he rowed a good deal in Boston Harbor.

He had long had an ambition to row to Egg Island and had selected this day for the trip. He had not asked Herbert to accompany him, being desirous of saying that he had accomplished the entire trip alone.

Though George had not seemed very friendly, Robert did not for a moment doubt that he would be willing to help him in his strait, and he was almost as delighted to see him as he would have been to see Herbert himself. There would be no need now of the raft, and he gladly suspended work upon it.

Rising to his feet, he called out:

"Hello, there!"

George paused in his rowing and asked—for he had not yet caught sight of Robert:

"Who calls?"

"I—Robert Coverdale!"

Then George, turning his glance in the right direction, caught sight of the boy he had tried to snub in the morning.

CHAPTER X

ROBERT COMPLETES THE RAFT

"What do you want of me?" asked George superciliously.

"Will you come to shore and take me into your boat?" asked Robert eagerly.

"Why should I? You have no claims on me," said George. "Indeed, I don't know you."

"I was at Mr. Irving's this morning, playing croquet with Herbert."

"I am aware of that, but that is no reason why I should take you into my boat. I prefer to be alone."

If Robert had not been in such a strait he would not have pressed the request, but he was not sure when there would be another chance to leave the island, and he persisted.

"You don't understand how I am situated," he said. "I wouldn't ask such a favor if I were not obliged to, but I have no other way of getting back. If you don't take me in, I shall probably be obliged to stay here all night."

"How did you come here?" asked George, his curiosity aroused.

"I came in a boat with my uncle."

"Then you can go back with him."

"He has gone back already. He is offended with me because I won't do something which he has no right to ask, and he has left me here purposely."

"Isn't your uncle a fisherman?"

"Yes."

"I don't care to associate with a fisherman's boy," said George.

Robert had never before met a boy so disagreeable as George, and his face flushed with anger and mortified pride.

"I don't think you are any better than Herbert," he said, "and he is willing to associate with me, though I am a fisherman's boy."

"I don't think much of his taste, and so I told him," said George. "My father is richer than Mr. Irving," he added proudly.

"Do you refuse to take me in your boat then?" asked Robert.

"I certainly do."

"Although I may be compelled to stay here all night?"

"That's nothing to me."

Robert was silent a moment. He didn't like to have any quarrel with Herbert's cousin, but he was a boy of spirit, and he could not let George leave without giving vent to his feeling.

"George Randolph," he broke out, "I don't care whether your father is worth a million; it doesn't make you a gentleman. You are a mean, contemptible fellow!"

"How dare you talk to me in that way, you young fisherman?" gasped George in astonishment and wrath.

"Because I think it will do you good to hear the truth," said Robert hotly. "You are the meanest fellow I ever met, and if I were Herbert Irving I'd pack you back to the city by the first train."

"You impudent rascal!" exclaimed George. "I've a good mind to come on shore and give you a flogging!"

"I wish you'd try it," said Robert significantly. "You might find yourself no match for a fisherman's boy."

"I suppose you'd like to get me on shore so that you might run off with my boat?" sneered George.

"I wouldn't leave you on the island, at any rate, if I did secure the boat," said Robert.

"Well, I won't gratify you," returned George, "I don't care to have my boat soiled by such a passenger."

"You'll get paid for your meanness some time, George Randolph."

"I've taken too much notice of you already, you low fisherman," said George. "I hope you'll have a good time staying here all night."

He began to row away, and as his boat receded Robert saw departing with it the best chance he had yet had of escape from his irksome captivity.

"I didn't suppose any boy could be so contemptibly mean," he reflected as his glance followed the boat, which gradually grew smaller and smaller as it drew near the mainland. "I don't think I'm fond of quarreling, but I wish I could get hold of that boy for five minutes."

Robert's indignation was natural, but it was ineffective. He might breathe out threats, but while he was a prisoner his aristocratic foe was riding quickly over the waves.

"He rows well," thought our hero, willing to do George justice in that respect. "I didn't think a city boy could row so well. I don't believe I could row any better myself, though I've been used to a boat ever since I was six years old."

But it would not do to spend all the afternoon in watching George and his boat or he would lose all chance of getting away himself before nightfall.

With a sigh he resumed work on the raft which he had hoped he could afford to dispense with and finally got it so far completed that he thought he might trust himself on it.

Robert was a little solicitous about the strength of his raft. It must be admitted that, though he had done the best he could, it was rather a rickety concern. If the nails had been all whole and new and he had had a good hammer and strong boards he could easily have made a satisfactory raft.

But the materials at his command were by no means of the best. The nails were nearly all rusty, some were snapped off in the middle and his stone did not work with the precision of a regular hammer.

"If it will only hold together till I can get to shore," he thought, "I won't care if it goes to pieces the next minute. It seems a little shaky, though. I must try to find a few more nails. It may increase the strength of it."

There was an end of a beam projecting from the sand, just at his feet.

Robert expected that probably he might by unearthing it find somewhere about it a few nails, and he accordingly commenced operations.

If he had had a shovel or a spade, he could have worked to better advantage, but as it was he was forced to content himself with a large shell which he picked up near the shore.

Soon he had excavated a considerable amount of sand and brought to the surface a considerable part of the buried beam. It was at this point that he felt the shell strike something hard.

"I suppose it is a stone," thought Robert.

And he continued his work with the object of getting it out of the way.

It was not long before the object was exposed to view.

What was Robert's surprise and excitement to find it an ivory portemonnaie, very much soiled and discolored by sea water!

Now, I suppose no one can find a purse or pocketbook without feeling his pulse a little quickened, especially where, as in Robert's case, money is so much needed.

He immediately opened the portemonnaie, and to his great delight found that it contained several gold pieces.

As my readers will feel curious to know the extent of his good luck, I will state definitely the amount of his discovery. There were two gold ten-dollar pieces, two of five, one two-dollar-and-a-half piece and fifty cents in silver. In all there were thirty-three dollars in gold and silver.

Robert's delight may be imagined. If he had felt in luck the day before, when he had been paid two dollars, how much more was he elated by a sum which to him seemed almost a fortune!

"I am glad George didn't take me on board his boat," he reflected. "If he had, I should never have found this money. Now, I don't care if I do stay here all night. Uncle had little idea what service he was doing me when he left me alone on Egg Island."

Though Robert expressed his willingness to spend the night on Egg Island, he soon became eager to get home so that he could exhibit to his aunt the evidence of his extraordinary luck.

He anticipated the joy of the poor woman as she saw assured to her for weeks to come a degree of comfort to which for a long time she had been unaccustomed.

Robert examined his raft once more and resolved to proceed to make it ready for service. It took longer than he anticipated, and it was nearly two hours later before he ventured to launch it. He used a board for a paddle, and on his frail craft he embarked, with a bold heart, for the mainland.

CHAPTER XI
A FRIEND GOES TO THE RESCUE

Leaving Robert for a time, we will accompany George Randolph on his homeward trip.

George did not at all enjoy the plain speaking he had heard from Robert. The more he thought of it the more his pride was outraged and the more deeply he was incensed.

"The low-lived fellow!" he exclaimed as he was rowing home. "I never heard of such impudence before. He actually seemed to think that I would take as a passenger a common fisherman's boy. I haven't sunk as low as that."

George was brought up to have a high opinion of himself and his position. He really thought that he was made of a different sort of clay than the poor boys with whom he was brought in contact, and his foolish parents encouraged him in this foolish belief.

Probably he would have been very much shocked if it had become known that his own grandfather was an honest mechanic, who was compelled to live in a very humble way.

George chose to forget this or to keep it out of sight, as it might have embarrassed him when he was making his high social pretensions.

Falsely trained as he had been, and with a strong tendency to selfishness, George had no difficulty in persuading himself that he had done exactly right in rebuking the forwardness of his humble acquaintance.

"He isn't fit to associate with a gentleman," he said to himself. "What business is it of mine that he has to stay on the island all night? If his uncle left him there, I dare say he deserved it."

George did not immediately land when he reached the beach, but floated here and there at will, enjoying the delightful sea breeze which set in from seaward. At length, however, he became tired and landed. The boat did not belong to him, but was hired of a fisherman living near by, who had an extra boat.

The owner of the boat was on hand when George landed. He was, though a fisherman, a man of good, sound common sense, who read a good deal in his leisure moments and was therefore well informed. Like many other New England men of low position, he was superior to his humble station and was capable of acquitting himself creditably in a much higher sphere. It is from persons of his class that our prominent men are often recruited.

It may be mentioned here that, though George's father, as he liked to boast, was a rich man, the boy himself was very mean in money matters and seldom willing to pay a fair price for anything. He was not above driving a close bargain, and to save five cents would dispute for half an hour.

"So you've got back young man?" said Ben Bence, the fisherman. "Did you have a pleasant trip?"

"Quite fair," answered George in a patronizing tone. "I rowed over to Egg Island and back."

"That's doing very well for a city boy," said the fisherman.

"I should think it was good for any boy or man either," said George, annoyed at this depreciation of his great achievement.

Bence laughed.

"Why," said he, "I'm out for four or five hours sometimes. I don't think anything of rowing from fifteen to twenty miles, while you have rowed only six."

"I don't expect to row as far as a man," said George, rather taken down.

"The best rower round here among the boys is Bob Coverdaie," said the fisherman.

"What can he do?" asked George with a sneer.

"He can row ten miles without feeling it," said Bence.

"Does he say so?" asked George in a meaning tone.

"No, but I have seen him do it. He's been out with me more than once. He's a muscular boy, Bob is. Do you know him?"

"I have seen him," answered George distantly.

"He's a great chum of your cousin, Herbert Irving," said Bence, "and so I thought you might have met him."

This subject was not to George's taste, and he proceeded to change it.

"Well, my good man," he said patronizingly, "how much do I owe you?"

"So I am your good man?" repeated Ben Bence with an amused smile. "I am much obliged to you, I am sure. Well, you were gone about two hours, I reckon."

"I don't think it was quite as much as that," said George.

"I guess twenty-five cents will about pay me."

"Twenty-five cents!" repeated George, all his meanness asserting itself. "I think that is a very high price!"

"Did you expect to get the boat for nothing?" asked the fisherman, surprised.

"Of course not. I wouldn't be beholden to a fisherman," George said haughtily.

"Indeed! How much did you calculate to pay?"

"I think twenty cents is enough."

"Then the only difference between us is five cents?"

"Yes."

"Then you can pay me twenty cents. I can live without the extra five cents."

George, pleased at gaining his point, put two ten-cent pieces in the hands of the owner of the boat, saying:

"I don't care about the five cents, of course, but I don't like to pay too much."

"I understand, Master Randolph," said the fisherman with a quizzical smile. "In your position, of course, you need to be economical."

21

"What do you mean?" asked George with a flushed face.

"Oh, nothing!" answered Ben Bence, smiling.

The smile made George uncomfortable. Was it possible that this common fisherman was laughing at him? But, of course, that did not matter, and he had saved his five cents.

George got home in time for supper, but it was not till after supper that he mentioned to Herbert:

"I saw that young fisherman this afternoon."

"What young fisherman?"

"The one you played croquet with this morning."

"Oh, Bob Coverdale! Where did you see him?" asked Herbert with interest.

"On Egg Island."

"How came he there?" inquired Herbert, rather surprised.

"He went there in a boat with his uncle. I expect he's there now."

"Why should he stay over there so long?"

"It's a rich joke," said George, laughing. "It seems his uncle was mad with him and landed him there as a punishment. He's got to stay there all night."

"I don't see anything so very amusing in that," said Herbert, who was now thoroughly interested.

"He wanted me to take him off," proceeded George. "He was trying to build a raft. I told him he'd better keep at it."

If George had watched the countenance of his cousin he would have seen that Herbert was very angry, but he was so amused by the thought of Robert's perplexity that he did not notice.

"Do you mean to say that you refused to take him off?" demanded Herbert in a quick, stern tone that arrested George's attention.

"Of course I did! What claim had he on me?"

"And you deliberately left him there, when it would have been no trouble to give him a passage back?"

"Really, Herbert, I don't like your way of speaking. It was my boat—or, at least, I was paying for the use of it—and I didn't choose to take him as a passenger."

"George Randolph, do you want to know my opinion of you?" asked Herbert hotly.

"What do you mean?" stammered George.

"I mean this, that I am ashamed of you. You are the most contemptibly mean fellow I ever met, and I am heartily sorry there is any relationship between us."

"I consider that an insult!" exclaimed George, pale with anger.

"I am glad you do. I mean it as such. Just tell my mother I won't be back till late in the evening."

"Where are you going?"

"I am going to get a boat and row to Egg Island for Bob Coverdale," and Herbert dashed up the street in the direction of the beach.

"He must be crazy!" muttered George, looking after his cousin.

Herbert Irving reached the beach and sought out Ben Bence.

"Mr. Bence," he said, "I want to go to Egg Island. If you can spare the time, come with me and I'll pay you for your time."

"What are you going for, Master Herbert?"

Upon this Herbert explained the object of his trip.

"Now, will you go?" he asked.

"Yes," answered the fisherman heartily, "I'll go and won't charge you a cent for the boat or my time. Bob Coverdale's a favorite of mine, and I'm sorry his uncle treats him so badly."

Strong, sturdy strokes soon brought them to the island.

"Bob! Where are you. Bob?" called Herbert.

There was no answer. The island was so small that he would have been seen if he had been there.

"He must have got off," said Herbert. "George said he was building a raft."

"Then I mistrust something's happened to the poor boy," said Bence gravely. "He couldn't build a raft here that would hold together till he reached the mainland."

Herbert turned pale.

"I hope it isn't so bad as that," he said. "Let us row back as quick as we can!"

CHAPTER XII

A MYSTERIOUS DISAPPEARANCE

As they were rowing back they scanned the sea in every direction, but nowhere did they discover any signs of Robert or his raft.

"Perhaps," suggested Herbert, breaking a long silence, "Bob is already at home."

He looked inquiringly in the face of his companion to see what he thought of the chances.

"Mayhap he is," said Ben Bence slowly, "but I mistrust he found it too rough for the raft."

"In that case——" said Herbert anxiously and stopped without answering the question.

"In that case the poor boy's at the bottom of the sea, it's likely."

"He could swim, Mr. Bence."

"Yes, but the tide would be too strong for him. Just about now there's a fearful undertow. I couldn't swim against it myself, let alone a boy."

"If anything has happened to him it's his uncle's fault," said Herbert.

"John Trafton will have to answer for it," said the fisherman sternly. "There ain't one of us that don't love Bob. He's a downright good boy, Bob Coverdale is, and a smart boy, too."

"If he's lost I will never have anything more to do with George Randolph. I will ask mother to pack him back to Boston to-morrow."

"George ain't a mite like you," said Ben Bence.

"I hope not," returned Herbert hastily. "He's one of the meanest boys I ever met. He might just as well have taken poor Bob off the island this afternoon, if he hadn't been so spiteful and ugly."

"It would serve him right to leave him there a while himself," suggested Bence.

"I agree with you."

There was another pause. Each was troubled by anxious thoughts about the missing boy. When they reached the shore Herbert said:

"I'm going to Mr. Trafton's to see if Bob has got home."

"I'll go with you," said the fisherman briefly.

They reached the humble cabin of the Traftons and knocked at the door.

Mrs. Trafton opened it.

"Good evening, Mr. Bence," she said. "I believe this young gentleman is Master Herbert Irving? I have often heard Robert speak of him."

"Is Robert at home?" asked Herbert eagerly.

"No, he has been away all day," answered his aunt.

"Do you know where he is?" inquired Ben Bence soberly.

"Mr. Trafton wouldn't tell me. He said he had sent him away on some errand, but I don't see where he could have gone, to stay so long."

It was clear Mrs. Trafton knew nothing of the trick which had been played upon her nephew.

"Tell her, Mr. Bence," said Herbert, turning to his companion.

"Has anything happened to Robert?" asked Mrs. Trafton, turning pale.

They told her how her husband had conveyed Robert to Egg Island and then treacherously left him there, to get off as he might.

"Was there any difficulty between Bob and his uncle?" asked Ben Bence.

"Yes; the boy had a little money which had been given him and my husband ordered him to give it up to him. He'd have done it, if he hadn't wanted to spend it for me. He was always a considerate boy, and I don't know what I should have done without him. Mr. Bence, I know it's a good deal to ask, but I can't bear to think of Robert staying on the island all night. Would you mind rowing over and bringing him back?"

As yet Mrs. Trafton did not understand that any greater peril menaced her nephew.

"Mrs. Trafton, we have just been over to Egg Island," said the fisherman.

"And didn't you find him?"

"No; he was not there."

"But how could he get off?"

"He was seen this afternoon making a raft from the old timbers he found in the wreck. He must have put to sea on it."

"Then why is he not here?"

"The sea was rough, and——"

Mrs. Trafton, who had been standing, sank into a chair with a startled look.

"You don't think my boy is lost?"

"I hate to think so, Mrs. Trafton, but it may be."

From grief there was a quick transition to righteous indignation.

"If the poor boy is drowned, I charge John Trafton with his death!" said the grief-stricken woman with an energy startling for one of her usually calm temperament.

"What's this about John Trafton?" demanded a rough voice.

It was John Trafton himself, who, unobserved, had reached the door of the cabin.

Ben Bence and Herbert shrank from him with natural aversion.

"So you're talking against me behind my back, are you?" asked Trafton, looking from one to the other with a scowl.

His wife rose to her feet and turned upon him a glance such as he had never met before.

"What have you done with Robert, John Trafton?" she demanded sternly.

"Oh! that's it, is it?" he said, laughing shortly. "I've served him as he deserved."

"What have you done with him?" she continued in a slow, measured voice.

"You needn't come any tragedy over me, old woman!" he answered with annoyance. "I left him on Egg Island to punish him for disobeying me!"

"I charge you with his murder!" she continued, confronting him with a courage quite new to her.

"Murder!" he repeated, starting. "Come, now, that's a little too strong! Leaving him on Egg Island isn't murdering him. You talk like a fool!"

"Trafton," said Ben Bence gravely, "there is reason to think that your nephew put off from the island on a raft, which he made himself, and that the raft went to pieces."

For the first time John Trafton's brown face lost its color.

"You don't mean to say Bob's drowned?" he ejaculated.

"There is reason to fear that he may be."

"I'll bet he's on the island now."

"We have just been there and he is not there."

At length Trafton began to see that the situation was a grave one, and he began to exculpate himself.

"If he was such a fool as to put to sea on a crazy raft it ain't my fault," he said. "I couldn't help it, could I?"

"If you hadn't left him there he would still be alive and well."

John Trafton pulled out his red cotton handkerchief from his pocket and began to wipe his forehead, on which the beads of perspiration were gathering.

"Of course I wouldn't have left him there if I'd known what he would do," he muttered.

"Did you mean to leave him there all night?" asked Bence.

"Yes, I meant it as a lesson to him," said the fisherman.

"A lesson to him? You are a fine man to give a lesson to him! You, who spend all your earnings for drink and leave me to starve! John Trafton, I charge you with the death of poor Robert!" exclaimed Mrs. Trafton with startling emphasis.

Perhaps nothing more contributed to overwhelm John Trafton than the wonderful change which had taken place in his usually gentle and submissive wife. He returned her accusing glance with a look of deprecation.

"Come now, Jane, be a little reasonable," he said. "You're very much mistaken. It was only in fun I left him. I thought it would be a good joke to leave him on the island all night. Say something for me, Ben—there's a good fellow."

But Ben Bence was not disposed to waste any sympathy on John Trafton. He was glad to see Trafton brought to judgment and felt like deepening his sense of guilt rather than lightening it.

"Your wife is right," he said gravely. "If poor Bob is dead, you are guilty of his death in the sight of God."

"But he isn't dead! It's all a false alarm. I'll get my boat and row over to the island myself. Very likely he had gone to sleep among the bushes and that prevented your seeing him."

There was a bare possibility of this, but Ben Bence had little faith in it.

"Go, if you like," he said. "If you find him, it will lift a great weight from your conscience."

John Trafton dashed to the shore, flung himself into his boat, and, with feverish haste, began to row toward the island. He bitterly repented now the act which had involved him in such grave responsibility.

He was perfectly sober, for his credit at the tavern was temporarily exhausted.

Of course those who remained behind in the cabin had no hope of Robert being found. They were forced to believe that the raft had gone to pieces and the poor boy, in his efforts to reach the shore, had been swept back into the ocean by the treacherous undertow and was now lying stiff and stark at the bottom of the sea.

"What shall I ever do without Robert?" said Mrs. Trafton, her defiant mood changing, at her husband's departure, to an outburst of grief. "He was all I had to live for."

"You have your husband," suggested Ben Bence doubtfully.

"My husband!" she repeated drearily. "You know how little company he is for me and how little he does to make me comfortable and happy. I will never forgive him for this day's work."

Ben Bence, who was a just man, ventured to represent that Trafton did not foresee the result of his action; but, in the sharpness of her bereavement, Mrs. Trafton would find no excuse for him.

Herbert, too, looked pale and distressed. He had a genuine attachment for Robert, whose good qualities he was able to recognize and appreciate, even if he was a fisherman's nephew.

He, too, thought sorrowfully of his poor friend, snatched from life and swept by the cruel and remorseless sea to an ocean grave. He, too, had his object of resentment.

But for George Randolph, he reflected, Robert would now be alive and well, and he resolved to visit George with his severest reproaches.

While all were plunged in a similar grief a strange thing happened.

The door of the cabin was closed by John Trafton as he went out.

Suddenly there was heard a scratching at the door, and a sound was heard as of a dog trying to excite attention.

"It must be my dog Dash," said Herbert. "I wonder how he found me out?"

He advanced to the door and opened it. Before him stood a dog, but it was not Dash. It was a large black dog, with an expression of intelligence almost human. He had in his mouth what appeared to be a scrap of writing paper. This he dropped on the ground when he saw that he had attracted Herbert's attention.

"What does this mean?" thought Herbert in great surprise, "and where does this dog come from?"

He stooped and picked up the paper, greatly to the dog's apparent satisfaction. It was folded in the middle and contained, written in pencil, the following message, which, not being directed to any one in particular, Herbert felt at liberty to read:

"Feel no anxiety about Robert Coverdale. He is safe!"

Herbert read the message, the dog uttered a quick bark of satisfaction, and, turning, ran down the cliff to the beach.

Herbert was so excited and delighted at the news of his friend's safety that he gave no further attention to the strange messenger, but hurried into the cabin.

"Mrs. Trafton—Mr. Bence!" he exclaimed, "Bob is safe!"

"What do you mean? What have you heard?" they asked quickly.

"Read this!" answered Herbert, giving Mrs. Trafton the scrap of paper.

"Who brought it?" she asked, bewildered.

"A dog."

Ben Bence quickly asked:

"What do you mean?"

"I know nothing more than that a large black dog came to the door with this in his mouth, which he dropped at my feet."

"That is very strange," said Bence.

He opened the door and looked out, but no dog was to be seen.

"Do you believe this? Can it be true?" asked Mrs. Trafton.

"I believe it is true, though I can't explain it," answered Ben. "Some dogs are wonderfully trained. I don't know whom this dog belongs to, but whoever it is he doubtless has Robert under his care. Let us be thankful that he has been saved."

"But why don't he come home?" asked Mrs. Trafton. "Where can he be?"

"He was probably rescued in an exhausted condition. Cheer up, Mrs. Trafton. You will no doubt see your boy to-morrow."

"I feel like giving three cheers, Mr. Bence," said Herbert.

"Then give 'em, boy, and I'll help you!" said old Ben.

The three cheers were given with a will, and Herbert went home, his heart much lighter than it had been ten minutes before.

CHAPTER XIII
THE CRUISE OF THE RAFT

It is time we carried the reader back to the time when Robert, after launching his rude raft, set out from the island of his captivity.

Notwithstanding his rather critical situation, he was in excellent spirits. The treasure which he had unearthed from the wreck very much elated him. It meant comfort and independence for a time at least, and in his new joy he was even ready to forgive his uncle for leaving him on the island and Randolph for not taking him off.

"I've heard of things turning out for the best," was the thought that passed through his mind, "but I never understood it so well before."

Robert possessed a large measure of courage and he had been used to the sea from the age of six, or as far back as he could remember, but when he had rounded the Island and paddled a few rods out to sea he began to feel serious.

There was a strong wind blowing, and this had roughened the sea and made it difficult for him to guide his extemporized raft in the direction he desired.

Had it been his uncle's fishing boat and had he but possessed a good pair of stout oars, he would have experienced no particular difficulty.

He would perhaps have found it rather hard pulling, but he was unusually strong for his age, and, in the end, he would have reached the shore. But with a frail raft, loosely put together, and only a board to row or paddle with, his progress was very slow.

He did make a little progress, however, but it was so little that, at the end of fifteen minutes, he seemed as far off from the little cabin on the cliff as ever.

"It's hard work," said Robert to himself. "I wish I had a boat. If it were smooth water, I could get along with a raft, but now——"

He stopped short, as the raft was lifted on the crest of a wave, and he nearly slid off into the water.

He looked back to the island and began to consider whether it would not be best, after all, to paddle back and trust to being taken off the next morning by some fisherman's boat.

No doubt that would have been the most sensible thing to do, but Robert was very reluctant to relinquish his project.

Had he not devoted several hours to constructing the raft he was trying to navigate and should he allow this time to be thrown away?

Again, the prospect of passing a night upon Egg Island was not very inviting. There was nothing to fear, of course, for the island was too small to be infested by wild animals or even snakes. He could no doubt sleep some, even if his bed were not very comfortable.

Robert looked back. By this time he was half a mile, at a rough guess, from Egg Island, and between his raft and the mainland there intervened probably two miles and a half of rough sea.

"If I can get within half a mile of shore," thought our young hero, "I won't care for the raft any longer. I will plunge into the waves and swim to the shore."

He looked toward the shore.

There, in plain view, was the humble cabin which he called home. Inside doubtless was his aunt, worrying perhaps about his absence.

"How delighted she will be when I tell her of the money I have found!" thought Robert joyfully. "Come, Bob, brace up now and push out boldly for home."

With his eyes fixed on the cabin, our young hero used his paddle with such energy that, in the course of half an hour or thereabouts, he was about a mile farther on his way.

He had gone half way, and though he was somewhat fatigued, he was strong and muscular, and the chances were that he would be able to hold out till he reached the boat landing.

But now a new danger threatened itself.

The assaults of the sea had strained heavily the raft, which he had not been able, for want of nails, to make strong and secure.

Robert's heart beat with quiet alarm as he realized that there was small chance of his frail craft holding together till he reached shore.

The danger was hardly realized before it came.

A strong wave wrenched apart the timbers, and Robert Coverdale found himself, without warning, spilled into the sea, a mile and a half from land.

Instinctively he struck out and began to swim, but the distance was great and he was impeded by his clothes.

Looking neither to the right nor to the left, but only straight ahead, he swam with all the strength there was left to him, but he found himself weakening after a while and gave himself up for lost.

CHAPTER XIV

THE HERMIT OF THE CLIFF

The last thing that Robert could remember was the singing of the waters in his ears and a weight as of lead that bore him downward with a force which he felt unable to resist.

But at the critical moment, when the doors of death seemed to be swinging open to admit him, he was firmly seized by a slender, muscular arm, extended from a boat shaped somewhat like an Indian canoe and rowed by a tall, thin man with white hair and a long white beard.

In the dusk our hero had not seen the boat nor known that help was so near at hand. But the occupant of the boat had, from a distance, seen the going to pieces of the raft, and appreciated the peril of the brave swimmer, and paddled his boat energetically toward him just in time to rescue him when already insensible.

Pale and with closed eyes lay Robert in the bottom of the boat. The old man—for so he appeared—rather anxiously opened the boy's shirt and placed his hand over his heart. An expression of relief appeared on his face.

"He will do," he said sententiously and turned his attention to the boat.

Half a mile from the cliff on which stood the fisherman's cabin was another, rising to a greater height.

To this the stranger directed his boat. He fastened it and then, raising our hero in his arms, walked toward the cliff.

There was a cavity as wide as a door, but less in height, through which he passed, lowering his head as he entered. Inside the opening steadily widened and became higher. This cavity was about ten feet above the sandy beach and was reached by a ladder.

On he passed, guided amid the darkness by a light from a lantern hanging from the roof. The front portion of the cavern seemed like a hall, through which a narrow doorway led into a larger room, which was furnished like the interior of a house. Upon a walnut table stood a lamp, which the stranger lighted. He took the boy, already beginning to breathe more freely, and laid him on a lounge, covered with a buffalo skin, at the opposite side of the apartment. From a shelf he took a bottle and administered a cordial to Robert, who, though not yet sensible, mechanically swallowed it.

The effect was almost instantaneous.

The boy opened his eyes and looked about him in bewilderment.

"Where am I?" he inquired.

"What can you remember?" asked the old man.

Robert shuddered.

"I was struggling in the water," he answered. "I thought I was drowning."

Then, gazing at the strange apartment and the majestic face of the venerable stranger, he said hesitatingly:

"Am I still living or was I drowned?"

He was not certain whether he had made the mysterious passage from this world to the next, so strange and unfamiliar seemed everything about him.

"You are still in life," answered the stranger, smiling gravely. "God has spared you, and a long life is yet before you if He wills."

"And you saved me?"

"Yes."

"How can I thank you? I owe you my life," said Robert gratefully.

"I am indebted to you for the opportunity once more to be of use to one of my race."

"I don't understand how you could have saved me. When I went down I could see no one near."

"On account of the dusk. I was not far away in my boat. I saw your peril and hastened to your assistance. Fortunately I was not too late. Do you know who it is that has saved you?"

"Yes," answered Robert.

"You have seen me before?"

"Yes, but not often."

"How do people call me?"

"They call you 'the hermit of the cliff.'"

"As well that as anything else," said the old man. "What more do they say of me?"

Robert seemed reluctant to tell, but there was something imperative in the old man's tone.

"Some say you are crazy," he answered.

"I am not surprised to hear it. The world is apt to say that of one who behaves differently from his fellows. But I must not talk too much of myself. How do you feel?"

"I feel weak," answered Robert.

"Doubtless. Swimming against such a current was a severe strain upon your strength. Let me feel your pulse."

He pressed his finger upon Robert's pulse and reported that the action was slow.

"It means exhaustion," he said. "You must sleep well, and to-morrow morning you will feel as well as usual."

"But I ought to go home," said Robert, trying to rise. "My aunt will feel anxious about me."

"Who is your aunt?"

"I am the nephew of John Trafton, who has a small house on the cliff."

"I know. He is a fisherman."

"Yes, sir."

"Don't disturb yourself. Word shall be sent to your aunt that you are safe. I will give you a sleeping draught, and tomorrow morning we will speak further."

Somehow Robert did not dream of resisting the will of his host. The old man had an air of command to which it seemed natural to submit. Moreover, he knew that to this mysterious stranger—the hermit of the cliff, as the fishermen called him—he was indebted for his life, and such a man must necessarily be his friend. Robert was, besides, in that condition of physical languor when, if he had felt disposed, he would have found it very difficult to make resistance to the will of another.

"First of all," said the old man, "you must take off your wet clothes. I will place them where they can dry, so that you may put them on in the morning."

With assistance Robert divested himself of his wet garments. As we know, he had little to take off. The stranger brought out a nightgown and then placed our hero in his own bed, wrapping him up in blankets.

"Now for the sleeping draught," he said.

From a bottle he poured out a few drops, which Robert swallowed. In less than three minutes he had closed his eyes and was in a profound slumber.

The old man regarded him with satisfaction as he lay breathing tranquilly upon the bed.

"He is young and strong. Nature has been kind to him and given him an excellent constitution. Sleep will repair the ill effects of exposure. I must remember my promise to the boy," he said.

Turning to the table, he drew from a drawer writing materials and wrote the brief message which, as we have already seen, was duly delivered, and then walked to the entrance of the cavern.

He placed a whistle to his lips, and in response to his summons a black dog came bounding to him from the recesses of the grotto and fawned upon him.

"Come with me, Carlo; I have work for you," he said.

The dog, as if he understood, followed his master out upon the beach.

They walked far enough to bring into clear distinctness the cabin on the cliff.

"Do you see that house, Carlo?" asked his master, directing the dog's attention with his outstretched finger.

Carlo answered by a short, quick bark, which apparently meant "yes."

"Carry this note there. Do you understand?"

The dog opened his mouth to receive the missive and trotted contentedly away.

The hermit turned and retraced his steps to the cavern. He stood beside the bed and saw, to his satisfaction, that Robert was still sleeping peacefully.

"It is strange," said he musingly, "that I should feel such an interest in this boy. I had forsworn all intercourse with my kind, save to provide myself with the necessaries of life. For two years I have lived here alone with my dog and I fancied that I felt no further interest in the affairs of my fellow men. Yet here is a poor boy thrown on my hands, and I feel positive pleasure in having him with me. Yet he is nothing to me. He belongs to a poor fisherman's family, and probably he is uneducated, and has no tastes in common with me. Yet he is an attractive boy. He has a well-shaped head and a bright eye. There must be a capacity for something better and higher. I will speak with him in the morning."

He opened a volume from his bookcase, to which reference has not as yet been made, and for two hours he seemed to be absorbed by it.

Closing it at length, he threw himself upon the couch on which Robert had at first been placed and finally fell asleep.

CHAPTER XV
THE HOME OF THE HERMIT

When Robert awoke the next morning he found himself alone. His strange host was absent, on some errand perhaps.

After a brief glance of bewilderment, Robert remembered where he was, and with the recovery of his strength, which had been repaired by sleep, he felt a natural curiosity about his host and his strange home.

So far as he knew, he was the first inhabitant of the village who had been admitted to a sight of its mystery.

For two years the hermit of the cliff had made his home there, but he had shunned all intercourse with his neighbors and had coldly repelled all advances and checked all curiosity by his persistent taciturnity. From time to time he went to the village for supplies, and when they were too bulky to admit of his carrying them, he had had them delivered on the beach in front of the entrance to his cave dwelling and at his leisure carried them in himself.

He always attracted attention, as with his tall, slender, majestic figure he moved through the village, or paced the beach, or impelled his frail boat. But speculation as to who he was or what had induced him to become a recluse had about ceased from the despair of obtaining any light upon these points.

No wonder then that Robert, admitted by chance to his dwelling, looked about him in curious wonder.

Cavern as it was, the room was fitted up with due regard to comfort and even luxury.

The bed on which our hero reposed was soft and inviting. The rough stone floor was not carpeted, but was spread with Turkish rugs. There was a bookcase, containing perhaps two hundred books; there was a table and writing desk, an easy-chair and a rocking-chair, and the necessarily dark interior was lighted by an astral lamp, diffusing a soft and pleasant light. On a shelf ticked a French clock and underneath it was a bureau provided with toilet necessaries.

No one in the village knew how these articles had been spirited into the cavern. No one of the villagers had assisted. Indeed, no one, except Robert, knew that the hermit was so well provided with comforts.

Our hero found his clothes on a chair at his bedside. They were drier and suitable for wearing.

"I may as well dress," thought Robert. "I won't go away till I've seen the hermit. I want to thank him again for taking such good care of me."

He did not have to wait long, however. He had scarcely completed his toilet when the hermit appeared.

"So, my young friend, you are quite recovered from your bath?"

"Yes, sir."

"That is well."

"I think, sir, I had better go home now, for my aunt will be anxious about me."

"I sent a message to your aunt last evening. She knew before she went to bed that you were safe."

"Thank you, sir!"

"I am not apt to be curious, but I wish, before you leave me, to ask you a few questions. Sit down, if you please."

Robert seated himself. He felt that the hermit had a right to ask some questions of one whom he had saved.

"How came you so far out at sea on a frail raft? If you had been shipwrecked, that would explain it, but as you have not been to sea, I cannot understand it."

"I found myself on Egg Island, without any means of getting off. So I made a raft from the timbers of the wreck and launched it. I thought it would last long enough for me to reach land."

"It was a hazardous enterprise. But how came you on the island? Surely you did not swim there?"

"No, sir. My uncle carried me there in his boat. He refused to take me off unless I would give up some money which I wanted to spend for my aunt."

"Was the money yours?"

"Yes, sir. It was given me by a gentleman living at the hotel."

"Your uncle—John Trafton—is not a temperate man?"

"No, sir. He spends all the money he earns on drink, and my aunt and I have to live as we can."

"What a fool is man!" said the hermit musingly. "He alone of created beings allows himself to be controlled by his appetites, while professing to stand at the head of the universe!"

Robert felt that he was not expected to answer this speech and remained respectfully silent till his host resumed his questioning.

"And you," said the old man abruptly, "what do you do?"

"Sometimes I go out with my uncle's boat and catch fish for use at home. Sometimes I find jobs to do in the village which bring in a little money. I am always glad of that, for we can't buy groceries without money, and my uncle never gives us any. My aunt is very fond of tea, but once for three weeks she had to do without it."

"That was a pity. There are some who find great comfort in tea."

"It is so with Aunt Jane. She says it puts new life in her."

"Have you any money now?"

"Oh, I forgot to tell you of my good luck!" said Robert eagerly. "Just before I left the wreck I dug up this," and he displayed the purse with the gold pieces in it. "It would have been a pity if I had been drowned with all this in my pocket."

"My poor boy, your young life would have outweighed a thousandfold the value of these paltry coins. Still I do not depreciate them, for they may be exchanged for comforts. But will not your uncle seek to take them from you?"

"He will not know that I have this money. I shall not tell him."

"It will be better."

For a brief time the hermit gazed at Robert in thoughtful silence and then said:

"How old are you?"

"Fifteen, sir."

"Have you ever thought of life and its uses—I mean of the uses of your own life? Have you ever formed plans for the future?"

"No, sir. It did not seem of much use. I have had to consider how to get enough for my aunt and myself to live upon."

"So your uncle's burdens have been laid on your young shoulders? Have you no aspirations? Are you willing to follow in his steps and grow up a fisherman, like your neighbors?"

"No, sir. I should be very sorry if I thought I must always live here at Cook's Harbor and go out fishing. I should like to see something of the world, as I suppose you have."

"Yes, I have seen much of the world—too much for my happiness—or I would not have come to this quiet spot to end my days. But for a young and guileless boy, whose life is but beginning, the world has its charms. Do you care for books?"

"I have never looked into many, sir, but that is not my fault. I have half a dozen tattered books at home and I study in some of them every day. I have been nearly through the arithmetic and I know something of geography. Sometimes I get hold of a paper, but not often, for my uncle takes none and does not care for reading."

"Look among my books. See if there is any one you would like to read."

Robert had already cast wistful glances at the rows of books in the handsome bookcase. He had never before seen so many books together, for Cook's Harbor was not noted for its literary men and book lovers. He gladly accepted the hermit's invitation.

His attention was quickly drawn to a set of the Waverley novels. He had often heard of them, and an extract which he had seen in his school reader from "Rob Roy" had given him a strong desire to read the story from which it was taken.

"I should like to borrow 'Rob Roy,'" he said.

"You may take it. When you have read it, you may, upon returning it, have another."

"Then I may call to see you, sir?"

"I shall be glad to have you do so. It is an invitation I never expected to give, but you have interested me, and I may be able to serve you at some time."

"Thank you, sir. If you should ever want any one to run errands for you, I hope you will call upon me. I should like to make some return for your great kindness."

"That is well thought of. You may come to me every Tuesday and Friday mornings, at nine o'clock, and carry my orders to the village. I do not care to go there, but have had no messenger I could trust. For this service I will pay you two dollars a week."

Robert was astonished at the mention of such liberal payment.

"But, sir, that is rather too much," he began.

"Let it be so," said the hermit. "I have money in plenty and it does not bring me happiness. In your hands it may do good."

"It will be a great help to me, sir."

"It is understood then. I will not detain you longer. Go home and gladden the heart of your aunt."

Robert left the cavern, more than ever puzzled by his brief acquaintance with the mysterious recluse.

CHAPTER XVI
THE FISHERMAN'S TEMPTATION

It is needless to say that Robert received a joyful welcome from his aunt. Her joy was increased when her nephew showed her the gold which he had found upon the island.

"You see, aunt," he said, "it wasn't such bad luck, after all, to be left on the island."

"God has so shaped events as to bring good out of evil," answered Mrs. Trafton, who was a religious woman and went regularly to church, though her husband never accompanied her. "But I am afraid your uncle will try to get the money away from you."

"I don't want him to know it, aunt."

"I shall not tell him, Robert, but he may find out."

"That is not all. I have got regular work to do which will bring me in two dollars a week."

Then Robert told his surprised aunt the story of his engagement by the hermit, who for two years had been the mystery of the village.

"It never rains but it pours, you see, aunt," he said cheerfully.

He wondered how his uncle would receive him and whether he would make a fresh demand for the small sum of money which had been the cause of the original trouble.

But John Trafton had been thoroughly alarmed by the consequences of his former act and he had, besides, such experience of Robert's firmness that he concluded it would not be worth while to carry the matter any further. He greeted Robert sullenly.

"So you are back?" he said gruffly.

"Yes," answered the boy.

"Who took you off?"

"I put off on a raft and should have been drowned but for the hermit. He saved me."

"You deserved to be drowned for putting off on a raft."

"Did you think I was going to stay on the island?" asked Robert with spirit. "If I had been drowned it would have been your fault."

"None of your impudence, boy!" said John Trafton.

And then he dropped the subject without referring to the money.

During the day Robert called on Herbert Irving to thank him for his interest in his behalf.

George was in the yard, but his valise was in his hand and he seemed on the point of departure. He scowled at Robert, but didn't speak.

"I'm glad to see you back, Bob," said Herbert warmly. "What an old rascal your uncle is! Now tell me all about how you escaped."

While Robert was telling the story the stage drove up and George got on board.

"Good-by, George!" said Herbert.

George did not deign a reply and rode sullenly away.

"He doesn't find that the climate of Cook's Harbor suits him," said Herbert significantly.

"He doesn't seem very happy about going," said Robert. "I didn't expect he would notice me, but he did not bid you good-by."

"The fact is George and I have had a flare-up," said Herbert. "I was disgusted with his heartlessness in refusing to take you from Egg Island, and I told him so pretty plainly. He accused me of insulting him and threatened to lay a complaint before my mother. I requested him to do so. Considerably to his surprise, she took my part and reproved him for his selfish and disagreeable pride. This was too much for the young gentleman, and he gave notice that he should return to the city. No one attempted to keep him, and he has felt compelled to carry out his threat, a good deal to his disappointment."

"I am sorry you are losing your visitor on my account, Herbert."

"You needn't. Though he is my cousin, I am glad to have him go."

"But you will feel lonely."

"Not if you come to see me every day, Bob."

"If we didn't live in a poor cabin, I would ask you to visit me."

"Never mind about how you live; I will come. It isn't the house I shall come to see, but you. Some time when you are going out fishing I wish you would take me along."

"With all my heart, if you will come."

To Herbert alone Robert confided his discovery of the purse of gold.

It was about a week before Robert had occasion to use any of his gold. By that time he had spent the balance of the money given him by Mr. Lawrence Tudor and was forced to fall back upon his gold, having as yet received nothing from the hermit, who knew that he was not in immediate want of money.

Abner Sands was standing behind the counter in his grocery when Robert entered.

"What can I do for ye, Robert?" asked the trader.

"You may give me two pounds of tea and six pounds of flour."

"I s'pose ye've got the money," said Sands cautiously.

"Of course I have."

"You're doin' well now, Robert, I take it?" said the trader.

"Better than I used to," answered Robert.

He did not choose to make a confidant of Mr. Sands, who was a man of great curiosity and an inveterate gossip.

When the goods were done up in separate parcels Robert took out the two-dollar-and-a-half gold piece and passed it to the grocer.

"Why, I declare, it's gold!" exclaimed Mr. Sands wonderingly.

"Yes, it is gold."

"Of all things, I didn't expect to get gold from you, Robert Coverdale. I reckon you've found a gold mine!"

"Perhaps I have," said Robert, smiling.

As he put his hand in his pocket another gold piece dropped to the floor and he picked it up hastily, provoked at his carelessness, not, however, before the astonished trader had seen it.

He was sorely puzzled to know how a poor boy like Robert could have so much money in his possession and put one or two questions, which our hero evaded.

"The tea and flour came to a dollar and a quarter," said the shrewd trader, "and that leaves a dollar and a quarter to come to you."

He tendered Robert a one-dollar bill and twenty-five cents.

After Robert went home Mr. Sands searched his brain in trying to guess where he could have obtained his gold, but the more he thought the darker and more mysterious it seemed. While in this state of perplexity John Trafton entered the store.

He had seen Robert going out with two large parcels, and he came in to learn what he could about them.

"How d'ye do, Sands?" he said. "Has Bob been in here?"

"Yes."

"Did he buy anything?"

"Two pounds of tea and half a dozen pounds of flour. Seems to have considerable money."

"Does he?" inquired Trafton eagerly.

"I thought you knew. Why, he paid me in gold!"

"In gold?" ejaculated Trafton.

"To be sure! He give me a two-and-a-half gold piece, and that wasn't all. He dropped a ten-dollar gold piece by accident, but picked it right up."

"You don't mean it?" said the fisherman, astounded.

"Yes, I do. But I s'posed you knew all about it."

"I only know what you've told me. The fact is that boy hasn't a spark of gratitude. It seems he's rolling in wealth and leaves me to get along as I can."

"Nephews ain't generally expected to provide for their uncles," said Abner Sands dryly.

But John Trafton did not hear him. As he left the store an idea entered his mind. He knew that Robert had found a friend in the hermit, and he decided that the gold came from him.

If that was the case, the hermit must be rich. Who knows but he might have thousands of dollars in the cave? The fisherman's eyes sparkled with greed and he was assailed by a powerful temptation. His credit at the tavern was about exhausted. What a pity he could not get some of the gold, which appeared to do its possessor so little good!

CHAPTER XVII
JOHN TRAFTON'S NEW PLAN

With the new but unlawful purpose which he had begun to entertain John Trafton resolved to find out all he could about the hermit, and he rightly judged that Robert could give him more information than anybody else.

He decided to go home early and question his nephew cautiously. If he could find out something about the hermit's habits and peculiarities it would help him in his plan, for there was no beating about the bush now.

He acknowledged to himself that he meant to enter the cave, and if he could only find the gold, which he was persuaded the occupant owned in large quantities, to enrich himself at his expense.

His imagination was dazzled at the prospect. All his life he had been working for a bare living. Probably, in his most prosperous year, not over three hundred dollars in money had come into his hands as the recompense of his toil.

Probably there are few people who do not, at some time, indulge in dreams of sudden wealth. This time had come to John Trafton, and, unfortunately, the temptation which came with it was so powerful as to confuse his notions of right and wrong and almost to persuade him that there was nothing very much out of the way in robbing the recluse of his hoards.

"It don't do him any good," argued the fisherman, "while it would make me comfortable for life. If I had ten thousand dollars, or even five, I'd go away from here and live like a gentleman. My wife should be rigged out from top to toe, and we'd jest settle down and take things easy."

John Trafton was not very strict in his principles, and his conscience did not trouble him much. Even if it had, the dazzling picture which his fancy painted of an easy and luxurious future would probably have carried the day.

It was only eight o'clock in the evening when the fisherman lifted the latch of the outer door and entered the cabin.

His wife and Robert looked up in surprise, for it was about two hours earlier than he generally made his appearance.

Another surprise—his gait and general appearance showed that he was quite sober. This was gratifying, even if it was the result of his credit being exhausted.

During the preceding week it may be mentioned that he had worked more steadily than usual, having made several trips in his boat, and had thus been enabled to pay something on his score at the tavern.

John Trafton sat down before the fire.

His wife was mending stockings by the light of a candle which burned on the table at her side and Robert was absorbed by the fascinating pages of Scott's "Rob Roy."

A side glance showed the fisherman how his nephew was employed, and, rightly judging where the book came from, he seized upon it as likely to lead to the questions he wanted to ask.

"What book have you got there, Bob?" he inquired.

"It Is a story by Sir Walter Scott, uncle."

"Never heard of him. Does he live in Boston?" asked Trafton.

"No, he was a Scotchman."

"Some Scotchmen are pretty smart, I've heard tell."

"Scott was a wonderful genius," said Robert, glowing with enthusiasm.

"I dare say he was," said the fisherman placidly. "Where did you get the book?"

"I borrowed it of the hermit."

This was the name which Robert used, for even now he had no knowledge of his mysterious friend's name.

"Has he got many books?"

"A whole bookcase full."

"He must be a rich man," suggested John Trafton with apparent carelessness.

"I think he is," said Robert, wondering a little at his uncle's newborn interest in his new acquaintance, but suspecting nothing of his design in asking the question.

"It stands to reason he must be," continued the fisherman. "He doesn't do anything for a living."

"No."

"Then, of course, he's got enough to live on."

"Besides, all his furniture is very nice," cried Robert, falling into the trap. "He seems not to mind money and talks as if he was always used to it."

"I s'pose he pays you for running of errands for him," said Trafton.

"Yes," answered Robert reluctantly, for he feared that his uncle would ask to have the money transferred to him. But the next words of Trafton reassured him.

"That's all right," he said. "You can spend the money as you please. I don't ask you for any of it."

"Thank you, uncle," said Robert warmly.

Mrs. Trafton regarded her husband in surprise. He was appearing in a character new to her. What could his sudden unselfishness mean?

"I only asked because I didn't want you to work for nothing, Bob," said his uncle, not wishing it to appear that he had any other motive, as his plan must, of course, be kept secret from all.

"I wouldn't mind working for nothing, uncle. It would be small pay for his saving my life," Robert said with perfect sincerity.

"He wouldn't want you to do it—a rich man like him," returned the fisherman complacently. "It's the only money he has to spend, except what he pays for victuals. I'm glad you've fallen in with him. You might as well get the benefit of his money as anybody."

"Uncle seems to think I only think of money," Robert said to himself with some annoyance. "I begin to like the hermit. He is very kind to me."

He did not give utterance to this thought, rightly deeming that it would not be expedient, but suffered his uncle to think as he might.

"Does the hermit always stay at home in the evening?" asked the fisherman after a pause.

"Sometimes he goes out in his boat late at night and rows about half the night. I suppose he gets tired of being alone or else can't sleep."

John Trafton nodded with an expression of satisfaction.

This would suit his plans exactly. If he could only enter the cave in one of these absences, he would find everything easy and might accomplish his purpose without running any risk.

It was clear to him now that the gold of which the trader spoke was given to his nephew by the hermit. He was justified in thinking so, as there was no other conceivable way in which

Robert could have obtained it. He coveted the ten-dollar gold piece, but he was playing for a higher stake and could afford to let that go for the present at least.

The fisherman lit his pipe and smoked thoughtfully.

His wife was not partial to the odor of strong tobacco, but tobacco, she reflected, was much to be preferred to drink, and if her husband could be beguiled from the use of the latter by his pipe then she would gladly endure it.

John Trafton smoked about ten minutes in silence and then rose from his chair.

"I guess I'll go out on the beach and have my smoke there," he said as he took his hat from the peg on which he had hung it on entering the cabin.

"You're not going back to the tavern, John?" said his wife in alarm.

"No, I've quit the tavern for to-night. I'll just go out on the beach and have my smoke there. I won't be gone very long."

When Trafton had descended from the cliff to the beach he took the direction of the hermit's cave.

Of course he had been in that direction a good many times, but then there was nothing on his mind and he had not taken particular notice of the entrance or its surroundings.

It was a calm, pleasant moonlight night and objects were visible for a considerable distance. Trafton walked on till he stood at the foot of the cliff containing the cave. There was the rude ladder leading to the entrance. It was short. It could be scaled in a few seconds, and the box or chest of gold, in whose existence Trafton had a thorough belief, could be found. But caution must be used. Possibly the hermit might be at home, and if he were, he would, of course, be awake at that hour. Besides, the cave was dark and he had no light.

"When I come I will bring matches and a candle," thought the fisherman. "I can't find the gold unless I can see my way. What a fool this hermit must be to stay in such a place when with his money he could live handsomely in the city! But I don't find fault with him for that. It's so much the better for me."

He turned his eyes toward the sea, and by the light of the moon he saw the hermit's slender skiff approaching. The old man was plainly visible, with his long gray hair floating over his shoulders as he bent to the oars.

"He mustn't see me," muttered the fisherman. "I had better go home."

CHAPTER XVIII

A DESPERATE CONFLICT

About eight o'clock the next evening John Trafton sat in the barroom at the tavern enjoying himself in the manner characteristic of the place.

All day long his mind had been dwelling upon the plan which he had so recently formed, and he felt a feverish desire to carry it out.

"One bold stroke," he said to himself, "and I am a made man. No more hard work for me. I will live like a gentleman."

It was rather a strange idea the fisherman had—that he could live like a gentleman on the proceeds of a burglary—but there are many who, like him, consider that nothing is needed but money to make a gentleman.

That very night John Trafton decided to make the attempt, if circumstances seemed favorable. He shrank from it as the time approached and felt that he needed some artificial courage. For this reason he visited the tavern and patronized the bar more liberally than usual.

Trafton had prudently resolved to keep his design entirely secret and not to drop even a hint calculated to throw suspicion upon him after the event.

But there is an old proverb that when the wine is in the wit is out, and, though the fisherman indulged in whisky rather than wine, the saying will apply just as well to the one as to the other.

Among the company present in the barroom was one man who had been in the village a day or two, but was a stranger to all present.

He was a short, powerfully made man, roughly dressed, with a low brow and quick, furtive eyes that had a look of suspicion in them.

He had naturally found his way to the tavern bar and proved himself a liberal patron of the establishment. Therefore the landlord—though he did not fancy the looks of his new guest—treated him with politeness.

Somehow the conversation on that particular evening drifted to the probable wealth of city people who made their homes at Cook's Harbor during the summer. It was afterward remembered that the roughly dressed stranger had introduced the subject in a casual way.

"It's my opinion," said Ben Barton, "that Mr. Irving is our richest man."

"What makes you think so, Ben?" asked the landlord.

"The way he lives partly. He's got everything that money can buy. Besides, I heard his boy say that his father's watch cost him five hundred dollars. Now, it stands to reason that a man don't wear a watch like that unless he's got the money to back it."

"There's something in that," the landlord admitted.

The stranger seemed interested.

"Does this Irving stay down here himself?" he asked.

"No, he only comes down Saturday to stay over Sunday."

"Does he have much silver in the house?"

"I don't know. Why?" inquired Ben Barton, turning a surprised look upon the stranger.

"Because a real, tiptop rich man generally has plenty of plate," answered the man after a pause.

"I guess he doesn't keep it down here," said Barton. "It's likely he's got plenty in the city."

The stranger shrugged his shoulders.

"Does his wife wear diamonds?" he asked.

"Not down here. There wouldn't be any occasion."

"Does he get his groceries here or in the city?"

"He sends them down here by express."

The stranger seemed to lose all interest in the Irving family.

Two or three summer residents were mentioned who were supposed to be rich, but it did not appear that any of them kept valuables at their summer homes.

John Trafton had not taken any part in the conversation hitherto, and if he had been prudent he would have continued to remain silent, but a man excited by drink is not likely to be discreet.

He broke silence when there came a lull in the discussion.

"There's one man you haven't mentioned," he said, "who keeps more money on hand than Mr. Irving or any one else you have spoken of."

"A man in the village here?" asked the landlord.

"He means you, Mr. Jones," said Ben Barton jocosely. "Ain't we all of us bringing you money every day? You ought to have a pile by this time."

"So I might if all that were owing me would pay up," retorted the landlord.

As Ben was one of his debtors, this was felt to be a fair hit, and there was a laugh at his expense.

"P'r'aps Trafton means himself," suggested Ben by way of diversion.

"I wish I did," said the fisherman. "Well, I may be rich some time; stranger things have happened."

"I can't think of any stranger thing than that," said Ben.

And the laugh now was at Trafton's expense, but he didn't seem to mind it.

By this time the general curiosity was aroused.

"Who is this rich man you're talkin' about, Trafton?" asked Sam Cummings.

"The hermit of the cliff," answered the fisherman.

There was a general rustle of surprise.

"What reason have you for saying that?" asked Mr. Jones, the landlord.

By this time, however, John Trafton began to suspects that he had been imprudent and he answered with a mysterious shake of the head:

"I've no call to tell you that, but I've got my reasons."

"Can't you tell us, John?" asked Ben Barton.

"I might, but I won't; but I stand by what I've said."

"Doesn't your boy do errands for the hermit?" asked the landlord.

"Suppose he does?"

"And he goes into the hermit's cave?"

"Perhaps he does and perhaps he doesn't."

"I know he does, for I was on the beach a day or two ago and I see him a-climbin' the ladder and goin' in," said Ben Barton.

"You'll have to ask him about that," said the fisherman.

"Whereabouts is his cave?" asked the stranger, who had listened intently to what had been said.

One of the party described its location fully.

"Then I've seen it," said the other. "I was walking on the beach this morning and I wondered what the ladder was for."

He asked various questions about the hermit and his mode of life, which excited no wonder, as the curiosity about the hermit was shared by all.

35

John Trafton allowed himself to say one thing more that increased this feeling.

"I won't tell all I know," he said, "but I can tell you this hermit lives like a prince. He's got handsomer furniture than there is in any house in Cook's Harbor."

No one had told the fisherman this, but he knew the statement would make a sensation and chose to embellish what he had heard from Robert.

"That's a strange idea to furnish a cave that way," said the stranger.

"It may be strange, but it's true."

"Do you think he keeps a good deal of money by him?" asked the stranger with evident interest.

John Trafton nodded significantly.

The conversation now drifted into other channels. The stranger ordered another glass of whisky and went out.

"Where is that man staying?" asked Cummings.

"Not here," answered the landlord. "I don't like his looks and don't care where he stays as long as he don't ask for a room here."

"You don't mind selling him drink, landlord?"

"Not as long as he's got money to pay. That's a different matter."

A few minutes later John Trafton left the tavern.

He had drunk considerable, but not enough to make him incapable of action. The drink excited him and nerved him for the task he had in view, for upon this very evening he had decided to force an entrance into the hermit's mysterious residence, and he hoped to be well paid for his visit.

He had to pass his own cabin on the way. He glanced toward it and saw a light shining through the window, but he took care to keep far enough away so that he might not be seen.

Half a mile farther and he stood opposite the cavern. There was the ladder making access to the cave easy. He looked for the hermit's boat, which was usually kept fastened near the entrance to the cave, and to his joy he saw that it was missing.

"The old man must be out in his boat," he said to himself. "All the better for me! If I am quick, I may get through before he gets back."

With a confident step he ascended the ladder and entered what might be called the vestibule of the cave.

He halted there to light the candle he had brought with him. He was bending over, striking the match against his foot, when he was attacked from behind and almost stunned by a very heavy blow.

He recovered himself sufficiently to grasp his assailant, and in an instant the two were grappling in fierce conflict.

"I never thought the old man was so strong," passed through the fisherman's mind as he found himself compelled to use his utmost strength against his opponent.

CHAPTER XIX

A TRAGEDY ON THE BEACH

It is hardly necessary to say that the man with whom the fisherman was engaged in deadly conflict was not the hermit. It was the stranger who, in the tavern, had manifested so much curiosity on the subject of the rich residents of Cook's Harbor.

He was a desperado from New York, who, being too well known to the police of that city, had found it expedient to seek a new field, where he would not excite suspicion.

He had arrived at the cave only a few minutes before the fisherman and had already explored the inner room in search of the large sum of money which Trafton had given him to understand the hermit kept on hand.

He had no candle, but he found a lamp and lighted it.

He was in the midst of his search when he heard the entrance of the fisherman. He concluded, very naturally, that it was the hermit, and he prepared himself for an attack.

He instantly extinguished the lamp and stole out into the vestibule. It was his first thought to glide by the supposed hermit and escape, but this would cut him off from securing the booty of which he was in quest.

He resolved upon a bolder course. He grappled with the newcomer, confident of easily overcoming a feeble old man, but, to his disagreeable surprise, he encountered a vigorous resistance far beyond what he anticipated.

Neither of the two uttered a word, but silently the fierce conflict continued.

"I must be weak if I cannot handle an old man," thought the professional burglar, and he increased his efforts.

"If he masters me and finds out who I am, I am lost!" thought John Trafton; and he, too, put forth his utmost strength.

The fisherman had the disadvantage in one respect. He was wholly unarmed and his opponent had a knife.

When he found that Trafton—who was of muscular build—was likely to gain the advantage, with a muttered oath he drew his knife and plunged it into his opponent's breast.

They were struggling just on the verge of the precipice, and Trafton, when he felt the blow, tottered and fell, his antagonist with him.

"The old fool's dead, and I must fly," thought the burglar.

With hasty step he fled along the sands till he came to a point where he could easily scale the cliff. Reaching the top, he walked quickly away from Cook's Harbor.

Half an hour later the hermit beached his boat, fastened it and proceeded to his quarters. He was plunged in thought and observed nothing till he stumbled against the fisherman's body.

"Some drunken fellow probably," he said to himself.

He lit a match, and, bending over, was horror-stricken to see the fixed features and the blood upon the garments of the unfortunate fisherman.

"There has been murder here! Who can it be?" he exclaimed.

He lit another match and took a closer look.

"As I live, it is Trafton, Robert's uncle!" he cried. "What mystery is here? How did the unhappy man come to his death?"

He was not long left to wonder alone, for Robert, as was not unusual with him, had been taking an evening stroll on the beach, and, seeing his employer, came up to speak to him.

"Good evening, sir," he said, as yet innocent of the sad knowledge which was soon to be his. "Is anything the matter?"

"Robert," said the hermit solemnly, "prepare yourself for a terrible surprise. A man has been killed and that man is——"

"My uncle!" exclaimed our hero in dismay.

"Yes, it is he!"

"How did it happen, sir?" asked Robert, a frightful suspicion entering his mind.

"I know no better than you, my boy. I have just arrived from an evening trip on the water. I was about to enter my quarters when I stumbled over your uncle's body."

"What could have brought him here?"

"I cannot tell, nor can I conjecture who killed him."

"It can't be he," thought Robert, dismissing his fleeting suspicion. "What shall I do, sir?" he asked, unprepared, with his boyish inexperience, to decide what to do under such terrible circumstances.

"Go and summon some of your neighbors to carry the poor man to his home. Meanwhile break the news to your aunt as you best can," said the hermit in a tone of quiet decision.

"But should I not call the doctor?"

"It will be of no avail. Your uncle is past the help of any physician. Go, and I will stay here till you return."

The startling news which Robert brought to the fishermen served to bring men, women and children to the spot where John Trafton lay, ghastly with blood.

Well known as he was, the sight startled and agitated them, and, in their ignorance of the real murderer, suspicion fastened upon the hermit, who, tall and dignified, with his white hair falling upon his shoulders, stood among them like a being from another world.

Trafton's habits were well known, but the manner of his death enlisted public sympathy.

"Poor John!" said Tom Scott. "I've known him, man and boy, for a'most fifty years, and I never thought to see him lying like this."

"And what will you do with his murderer?" asked his wife in a shrill voice.

Mrs. Scott was somewhat of a virago, but she voiced the popular thought, and all looked to Scott for an expression of feeling.

"He ought to be strung up when he's found," said Scott.

"You won't have to look far for him, I'm thinkin'," said Mrs. Scott.

"What do you mean, wife?" asked Scott, who was not of a suspicious turn.

"There he stands!" said the virago, pointing with her extended finger to the hermit.

As this was a thought which had come to others, hostile eyes looked upon the hermit, and two or three moved forward as if to seize him.

The old man regarded the fishermen with surprise and said with dignity:

"My friends, what manner of man do you think I am that you suspect me of such a deed?"

"There's no one could have done it but you," said a young man doggedly. "Here lies Trafton at the foot of your ladder, with no one near him but you. You was found with him. It's a clear case."

"To be sure!" exclaimed two or three of the women. "Didn't Robert find you here, standin' by the dead body of his uncle?"

The hermit turned to our hero, who stood a little in the background, and said quietly:

"Robert, do you think I killed your uncle?"

"I am sure you didn't," said Robert, manfully meeting the angry glances which were now cast upon him.

"I am glad to have one friend here," said the hermit—"one who judges me better than the rest of my neighbors."

"He doesn't know anything about you and he's only a boy!" said Mrs. Scott, thrusting herself forward with arms akimbo. "I allus said there was something wrong about you or you wouldn't hide yourself away from the sight of men in a cave. Like as not you've committed murder before!"

"My good woman," said the hermit with a sad smile, "I am sorry you have so poor an opinion of me."

"Don't you call me good woman!" said Mrs. Scott, provoked. "I'm no more a good woman than yourself! I tell you, friends and neighbors, you'll do wrong if you let this man go. We may all be murdered in our beds!"

She was interrupted by the arrival of Mrs. Trafton, who had not been apprised of the tragedy from considerations for her feelings, but hearing the stir and excitement, had followed her neighbors to the spot and just ascertain what had happened.

"Where is my husband?" she cried.

All made way for her, feeling that hers was the foremost place, and she stood with startled gaze before her dead husband. Ill as he had provided for her and unworthy of her affections as he had proved, at that moment she forgot all but that the husband of her youth lay before her, bereft of life, and she kneeled, sobbing, at his side.

The hermit took off his hat and stood reverently by her side.

"Oh, John!" she sobbed, "I never thought it would come to this! Who could have had the heart to kill you?"

"That's the man! He murdered him!" said Mrs. Scott harshly, pointing to the hermit.

The widow lifted her eyes to the man of whom she had heard so much from Robert with a glance of incredulity.

He was too proud to defend himself from the coarse accusation and returned her look with a glance of sympathy and compassion.

"I never can believe that!" said the widow in utter incredulity. "He has been kind to my boy. He never would lift his hand against my husband!"

The hermit looked deeply gratified.

"Mrs. Trafton," he said, "you are right. I had no cause to harm your husband, nor would I have killed him for Robert's sake, whatever wrong he might have done me. But, in truth, I know of no reason why I should seek to injure him."

"If you are an innocent man," persisted Mrs. Scott, "tell us who you are and what brought you here."

"Yes, tell us who you are!" echoed two others who had always felt curious about the hermit.

"I do not choose to declare myself now," said the hermit gravely. "The time may come when I shall do so, but not now."

"That's because you're a thief or murderer!" exclaimed Mrs. Scott, exasperated.

"Wife, you're goin' too far!" said her husband.

"Mind your own business, Tom Scott!" retorted his wife in a tone with which he was only too familiar. "You ought to be ashamed of yourself tryin' to screen the murderer of your next-door neighbor."

"I am doing nothing of the kind. There's no proof that the hermit of the cliff murdered John Trafton."

"You must be a fool if you can't see it," said Mrs. Scott.

Robert Coverdale was shocked to hear his friend so abused and he said boldly:

"Mrs. Scott, I don't know who murdered my poor uncle, but I know the hermit did not. He has been a good friend to me, and he is no murderer."

"Go home and go to bed, boy!" said Mrs. Scott violently. "You take that man's part against your poor uncle."

Robert was provoked and answered with energy:

"I would sooner suspect you than him. I never heard the hermit say a word against my uncle, while only yesterday you called him a drunken vagabond."

This so turned the tables on Mrs. Scott that she was unable to return to the attack.

38

"Well, if I ever!" she ejaculated. "Tom Scott, are you goin' to see your wife sassed by a boy?"

"It seems to me, wife, that the boy is in the right in this instance," answered Tom, who had a sense of justice.

"So you turn against your lawful wife, do you?" exclaimed Mrs. Scott violently. "I'll come up with you yet. See if I don't."

Tom Scott shrugged his shoulders with resignation.

"I've no doubt you will," he answered with a half smile.

"My friends," said the hermit with calm dignity, "as it appears that some of you suspect me of this dastardly deed, I am quite willing to submit to any restraint you may desire till the groundlessness of the charge appears. You may leave a guard here in the cave or I will accompany you to any of your own houses. I certainly have no desire to escape while such suspicions are entertained."

Robert indignantly protested against such a step, but the hermit stayed his words.

"Robert," he said, "it is better. It will do me no harm, and, under the circumstances, while the matter is involved in mystery, I admit that it is perfectly justifiable and proper. My friends, I am in your hands. What will you do with me?"

Mrs. Scott expressed her opinion that he should be strung up immediately, but no one seconded her.

It was decided that two of the fishermen should remain at the cave that night to prevent any attempt at escape on the part of the hermit.

The body of the murdered fisherman was carried to his own cabin and properly cared for till the coroner, who must be brought from a neighboring town, should make his appearance.

CHAPTER XX
MR. JONES MAKES A CALL

When morning dawned a new face was put upon the matter. Steps were discovered leading from the scene of the murder along the beach and up the cliff. There were also discovered signs of a struggle in the cave, and it became clear that there had been a conflict and that one of the two concerned had escaped.

Of course it could not have been the hermit, for he was now in custody. Moreover, a fisherman who had been out in his boat in the evening remembered meeting the hermit rowing at about the time the murder must have been committed.

These discoveries cleared the hermit, but the question arose:

"Who was this other man?" There was no difficulty in solving this question. There were plenty who remembered the stranger who had spent a part of the previous evening in the barroom of the tavern, and his evident curiosity as to the wealth of the hermit was also remembered.

The real state of the case was now pretty well understood. This stranger had suddenly resolved to rob the hermit and had secretly found his way to the cavern.

But how did he happen to find the fisherman there and what was the object of the latter?

Then it was remembered that Trafton also had seemed much interested in the supposed hoards of the hermit, and, when his own want of money was considered, it was suspected that he, too, went on an errand similar to the burglar.

But he was dead, and his neighbors, who knew that he must have yielded to the force of a sudden and new temptation, did not care to speculate upon his object.

They were disposed to spare their old neighbor and charitably drop a veil over his attempted crime, which had brought upon him such fearful retribution.

Of course the hermit was released from custody, and there was not a person in the village who did not acquit him of all wrong except Mrs. Scott, who could not forgive him for proving her suspicions groundless.

"You may say what you will," she said perversely, "I know the man's a burglar, or a murderer, or something else bad."

"He couldn't have murdered John Trafton, for we traced the murderer's steps on the beach. There is no doubt it was that stranger we saw in the barroom."

So said her husband.

"I don't care whether he murdered John Trafton or not," said Mrs. Scott. "I'm sure he's murdered somebody, and I'm ready to take my Bible oath of it."

"What makes you so prejudiced against the poor man? He hasn't done you any harm, Mrs. Scott."

"I don't like the airs he puts on. He looks at you jest as if you were dust beneath his feet. What right has he to look down upon honest people, I want to know?"

But Mrs. Scott did not succeed in creating a prejudice against the hermit, whose courageous and dignified bearing had impressed all who observed his manner in this trying crisis.

When the funeral was over the hermit called in the evening upon the widow of John Trafton. It was the first he had ever made upon any of his neighbors and it excited surprise.

Robert brought forward the rocking-chair and invited the visitor cordially to sit down.

"Mrs. Trafton," said the hermit, "I want to thank you and Robert for the confidence you showed in me at a time when all others suspected me of a terrible deed. You were the ones most affected, yet you acquitted me in your hearts."

"Just for a moment I suspected you when I saw you standing by the dead body of my uncle," said Robert, "but it was only for a moment."

"I respect you for your fearless candor, my boy. You were justified in your momentary suspicion."

"I am ashamed of it. You had been such a kind friend."

"It was only natural. And now, my friends, what are your plans? How will you be able to maintain yourselves?"

"I don't think it will make much difference," began Robert hesitatingly.

"My husband did very little for our support," said Mrs. Trafton. "Not more, certainly, than his own food amounted to. You know, sir, I think Robert must have told you the unfortunate habits of my poor husband. He was enslaved by drink, and he spent nearly all he earned in the barroom."

"Yes, I knew what your husband's habits were," said the hermit gently. "It is a great pity he could not have lived to change them."

"I am afraid he never would," said the widow.

"They had grown upon him from year to year, and he seemed to get weaker and weaker in purpose."

"I had a brother who was equally unfortunate," said the hermit. "There are few families who are wholly free from the evils of intemperance. But have you formed any plans?"

"I suppose we can get along as we have," answered Mrs. Trafton. "With what you kindly pay Robert, and what he can pick up elsewhere, and the sewing I do, I think we can get along."

"Do you own this cottage?" inquired the hermit.

"Yes, sir."

"Then you will have no rent to pay."

"No, I don't know how we could do that."

The hermit looked thoughtful.

"I will see you again," he said as he rose to go.

On the whole, Mrs. Trafton and Robert were likely to get along as well as before John Trafton's death. Robert could use his uncle's boat for fishing, selling what they did not require, while regularly every week two dollars came in from the hermit.

It was a great source of relief that no rent must be paid. The fisherman's cabin and lot originally cost about five hundred dollars and the household furniture was of little value. The taxes were small and could easily be met. So there seemed nothing to prevent their living on in the same way as before.

Some time Robert hoped and expected to leave Cook's Harbor. He was a smart, enterprising, ambitious boy, and he felt that he would like a more stirring life in a larger place.

He was not ashamed of the fisherman's business, but he felt qualified for something better. It did not escape his notice that most of his neighbors were illiterate men, who had scarcely a thought beyond the success of their fishing trips, and he had already entered so far into the domain of study and books as to feel the charm of another world—the great world of knowledge—which lay spread out before him and beckoned him onward. But he was not impatient.

"My duty at present," he reflected, "Is to stay in Cook's Harbor and take care of my aunt. I am young and strong, and I don't mean that she shall want for any comforts which I can get for her."

He soon learned, however, that there was one great mistake in his calculations.

Robert was sitting by the door reading, after his return from a fishing trip, about a week after his uncle's funeral, when he heard the steps of some one approaching.

Looking up, he saw advancing toward their humble residence the stout, ponderous figure of Nahum Jones, the landlord of the village inn.

It was not often that Mr. Jones found his way to the beach. Usually he kept close to the tavern, unless he rode to some neighboring town. Therefore Robert was surprised to see him.

Nahum Jones nodded slightly, and, taking off his straw hat, wiped the perspiration from his forehead.

"Here, you, Bob," he said, "Is your aunt at home?"

"Yes, sir!" answered Robert, but not cordially, for he felt that Mr. Jones had been no friend of his uncle.

"Well, tell her I've come to have a talk with her, do you hear?"

"Yes, I hear," answered the boy coolly.

He rose from his chair and entered the house.

"Aunt Jane," he said, "here is Mr. Jones come to see you."

"What? The tavern keeper?" asked his aunt in great surprise.

"Yes, aunt."

"What can that man want of me?"

The question was answered, not by Robert but by Nahum Jones himself.

"I want to have a little talk with you, ma'am," said the burly landlord, entering without an invitation and seating himself unceremoniously.

"I will listen to what you have to say, Mr. Jones," said the widow, "but I will not pretend that I am glad to see you. You were an enemy to my poor husband."

"I don't know what you mean, Mrs. Trafton. Did he ever tell you that I was his enemy?"

"No, but it was you who sold him liquor and took the money which he should have spent on his own family."

"All nonsense, ma'am. You women are the most unreasonable creatures. I didn't ask him to drink."

"You tempted him to do it."

"I deny it!" said the landlord warmly. "I couldn't refuse to sell him what he asked for, could I? You must be a fool to talk so!" said the landlord roughly.

"I'll trouble you to speak respectfully to my aunt, Mr. Jones," said Robert with flashing eyes.

"Mind your own business, you young rascal!" said Nahum Jones, whose temper was not of the best.

"I mean to," retorted Robert. "My business is to protect my aunt from being insulted."

"Wait till you're a little bigger, boy," said Jones with a sneer.

Robert involuntarily doubled up his fist and answered:

"I mean to protect her now."

"Mrs. Trafton," said Nahum Jones, highly irritated, "you'd better silence that young cub or I may kick him out of doors!"

"You appear to forget that you are not in your own house, Nahum Jones," said the widow with dignity. "My nephew has acted perfectly right and only spoke as he should."

"So you sustain him in his impudence, do you?" snarled Jones, showing his teeth.

"If that is all you have come to say to me, Mr. Jones, you may as well go."

"By George, ma'am, you are mighty independent!"

"I am not dependent on the man who ruined my poor husband."

"No, but you're dependent on me!" exclaimed the landlord, pounding the floor forcibly with his cane.

"Will you explain yourself, sir?"

"I will," said Mr. Jones emphatically. "You talk about my not being in my own house, but it's just possible you are mistaken."

"What do you mean?" asked Mrs. Trafton, startled.

"I mean this, that I hold a mortgage on this house for two hundred dollars, and that's as much as it will fetch at auction. What do you say to that?"

Robert looked and felt as much troubled as his aunt. On his young shoulders fell this new burden, and he was at an utter loss what could be done.

"I thought I'd shut you up, you young cub!" said the landlord, glancing maliciously at Robert.

"You haven't shut me up!" retorted Robert with spirit.

"What have you got to say, hey?"

"That you ought to be ashamed to take all my uncle's earnings and then steal his home. That's what I've got to say!"

"I've a great mind to give you a caning," said Mr. Jones in a rage.

"You'd better not!" said Robert.

He was as tall as the landlord, and though not as strong, considerably more active, and he did not feel in the least frightened.

Nahum Jones was of a choleric disposition, and his face was purple with rage, but he hadn't yet said all he intended.

"I give you warning, Mrs. Trafton," he said, shaking his cane at our hero, "that I'm going to foreclose this mortgage and turn you into the street. You've got yourself to thank, you and this young rascal. I came here thinking I'd be easy with you, but I don't mean to stand your insulting talk. I'll give you four weeks to raise the money, and if you don't do it, out you go, bag and baggage. Perhaps when you're in the poorhouse you may be sorry you didn't treat me better."

"Oh, Robert, what shall we do?" asked the poor woman, her courage failing as she reflected on the possibility that the landlord's prediction might be fulfilled.

"Don't be alarmed, Aunt Jane; I'll take care of you," said Robert more cheerfully than he felt.

"Oh, you will, will you?" sneered Mr. Jones. "Anybody'd think to hear you that you were worth a pile of money. If your aunt depends on you to keep her out of the poorhouse, I would not give much for her chance."

"You won't have the satisfaction of seeing either of us there," said Robert defiantly.

"You needn't expect my wife to give you any more sewing," said Mr. Jones, scowling at the widow.

"I don't think my aunt wants any, considering she hasn't been paid for the last work she did," said Robert.

"What do you mean by that? I credited your uncle with twenty-five cents on his score."

"Without my aunt's consent."

Mr. Jones was so incensed at the defiant mien of the boy that he rocked violently to and fro—so violently that the chair, whose rockers were short, tipped over backward and the wrathful landlord rolled ignominiously on the floor.

"Here's you hat, Mr. Jones," said Robert, smiling in spite of himself as he picked it up and restored it to the mortified visitor.

"You'll hear from me!" roared the landlord furiously, aiming a blow at Robert and leaving the room precipitately. "You'll repent this day, see if you don't!"

After he had left the room Robert and his aunt looked at each other gravely. They had made an enemy out of a man who could turn them out of doors.

The future looked far from bright.

CHAPTER XXI

THE HERMIT'S SECRET

Mr. Jones, in his anger at Robert, regretted that he must wait four weeks before he could turn him and his aunt out of the house. It would be a great satisfaction to him to see the boy without a roof to shelter him, reduced to becoming a tramp or to take refuge in the poorhouse.

"By George, I'll humble the young beggar's pride!" exclaimed Mr. Jones as he hastened homeward from his unsatisfactory interview.

It must be admitted that Robert had not been exactly respectful, but, on the other hand, it is quite certain that the landlord had been rude and rough in manner and speech.

Why, then, did not Mr. Jones foreclose the mortgage instantly and gratify his resentment? Because in the instrument there was a proviso requiring a notice of four weeks.

However, he felt that it would make little difference.

"They can't raise the money in four weeks," he reflected. "There's nobody round here who will lend them the money, and they don't know anybody anywhere else."

So, on the whole, he was satisfied. Four weeks would soon pass, and then his thirst for revenge would be sated.

"What makes you so sober, my boy?" asked the hermit when Robert made his regular call upon him the next day.

"I feel anxious," answered the boy.

"But why need you? You told me your uncle did very little for the family. I think you will be able to take care of your aunt. If not, I will help you more."

"Thank you, sir; you are very kind. But we thought when you called the other day that we owned the house and would have no rent to pay."

"Were you mistaken about this?" asked the hermit quickly.

"It seems so. Mr. Jones, the tavern keeper, has a mortgage on the property and threatens to foreclose in four weeks unless the money is paid. Of course, we can't pay him, and I suppose we shall be turned out."

"How large is this mortgage?"

"Two hundred dollars."

"That is not a very great sum."

"It is very large to us. You know how poor we are."

"But have you no friend who will lend you the money?"

42

"No, sir."

"Are you sure of that?" asked the hermit with a peculiar smile, which inspired new hope in Robert. Then, without waiting for a reply, the man continued:

"If you are willing, I will pay this mortgage when the time comes, and I will be your creditor instead of Mr. Jones."

"How can I thank you?" exclaimed Robert joyfully. "My aunt will be delighted."

"Tell her then, but no one else. It will give Mr. Jones a surprise."

"It won't be a pleasant one. He was very rude and impolite and said he hoped to see us in the poorhouse."

"I don't believe you will ever go there, Robert," said the hermit, looking earnestly at the strong, energetic face of the boy before him.

"No, sir, I don't believe we will. But you are doing a great deal for us, sir. How can I ever repay you? If there was anything I could do for you I should be glad."

"Perhaps you can," said the hermit in a musing tone.

"Let me know what it is, sir, and I'll be glad to do it."

"Have you ever wondered," asked the hermit abruptly, "why I have left the haunts of men and retired to this out-of-the-way spot?"

"Yes, sir. I have thought of that often."

"Your curiosity is natural. I am not a poor man—in fact I should be called rich. Poverty and pecuniary troubles, therefore, have nothing to do with my strange act—as the world considers it. In my life there have been two tragedies. I was married, at the age of thirty, to a very beautiful young lady, whom I tenderly loved. I made my home in a city of considerable size and lived as my means warranted. One evening, as my wife stood before the open grate, dressed for a party, her dress caught fire, and before help could arrive she was fatally injured. Of course the blow was a terrible one. But I had a child—a boy of five—on whom my affections centered. A year later he mysteriously disappeared, and from that day I have never heard a word of him. When search proved unavailing, I became moody and a settled melancholy took possession of me. I could not endure the sight of other parents happy in the possession of children, and I doomed myself to a solitary life, wandering here and there till, two years since, I chanced to find this cave and made my home here."

"How old would your son be now?" asked Robert with interest.

"About your own age—perhaps a little older. It was this and a fancied resemblance which attracted me toward you."

"Had you any suspicion that your son was stolen?" asked Robert.

"Yes. In particular I suspected a cousin who would be my probable heir in case my boy died. But I could never prove anything, and the man expressed so much sympathy that I was ashamed to avow any suspicions. But Charles Waldo was a covetous man, insatiable in his greed of money and absolutely cold and unsympathetic, though his manner was plausible. He hoped that this second blow would kill me, but he has been disappointed."

"If the boy is living, perhaps he knows where he is," said Robert.

"If he abducted him—yes. He would not kill him, for he is too cautious a man and has too great fear of the law."

"Where is Mr. Waldo now living?"

"In Ohio. He has a large farm and a moderate amount of money invested—some twenty thousand dollars perhaps—so that he is able to live at ease. He was disappointed because I would not give him the charge of my property, but with the lingering suspicion in my mind I could not make up my mind to do it. He also sought a loan of ten thousand dollars, which I refused."

"How then does he expect to be your heir?" asked Robert.

"Two-thirds of my property is entailed and must be left to him if my boy is dead."

"If he really stole your son, he must be a wicked man," said Robert with boyish indignation at the thought.

"Yes, for he has wrecked two lives—mine and my boy's."

"Have you no hope of ever again seeing your son?"

"Only a slight one. I have thought of a plan in which I need your help."

"If I can help you, sir," said Robert heartily, "I will do so gladly."

"I do not doubt it, Robert," said the hermit kindly. "I will explain my meaning. If Charles Waldo knows anything of my lost boy, he must, from time to time, hold communication with him, and if he is watched he may some day reveal his hiding place."

"Why do you not go out to where he lives and watch him?"

"It would do no good. It would only put him on his guard. I intend this office for you."

"For me?" exclaimed Robert in amazement.

43

"Yes, you are young, but you have natural ability, and shrewdness. At any rate, you are the only one I have to send. It is a desperate chance, but I shall feel better satisfied when I have tried it."

"I will follow your instructions whenever you wish," said Robert, his heart beating at the prospect of seeing something of that world of which he had seen so little and heard so much.

"My instructions will be few. I must trust much to your shrewdness. You will need to visit the town where my cousin lives to observe his habits and any unusual visitors he may have—in fact, try to arrive at the knowledge of the secret, if there is one, connected with my boy's disappearance."

"What was your son's name?"

"Julian Huet. My own name is Gilbert Huet, but this information is for your ear alone."

"I will not mention it, sir."

"You need not feel anxious about leaving your aunt. I will see that her wants are provided for during your absence."

"Thank you, sir."

"And the mortgage shall be paid when it comes due."

"I wish I could be here to see Mr. Jones disappointed."

"You can hardly be back so soon. It may take you six months. The task is one that will require time. By the way, I do not wish you to mention to your aunt the nature of your errand. Merely tell her that you are traveling on business for me."

"Very well, sir. How soon do you wish me to start?"

"At the beginning of next week."

"I am afraid, sir, I have no clothes that are fit to wear," said Robert with hesitation.

"You will provide yourself in Boston with a suitable outfit. You will be supplied with an ample sum of money, and I will instruct my bankers to honor any drafts you may make."

"You will be spending a great deal of money for me, Mr. Huet."

"I am rich, and living as I have each year this made me richer. I will not grudge ten, twenty, fifty thousand dollars if you find my boy or bring me a clew which will lead to his discovery."

Robert was dazzled. It was evident that the hermit must be very rich. He walked home in high spirits. He was on the eve of an exciting journey and he enjoyed the prospect.

CHAPTER XXII

TWO PERSONS ARE SURPRISED

"Aunt," said Robert, his face aglow with excitement, "I am going to make a journey. I hope you won't feel lonely while I am away."

"A journey!" exclaimed Mrs. Trafton in astonishment.

"Yes, I am going away on business for the hermit."

"Where are you going?"

"To Boston first."

"To Boston? Land's sake! How can a boy like you find your way round in such a great city as Boston?"

"A boy of my age ought to be able to take care of himself."

"Why, child, you'll lose your way! There's ever so many streets and roads. I went to Boston once, and I got so puzzled I didn't know whether I stood on my head or my heels. If there was some older person going with you, now——"

"Aunt, don't make a baby of me. I guess I can get along as well as anybody."

"Well, you can try it. When will you be back?"

"When I get my business done."

"You won't be gone over two days, I calculate."

"I may be gone two months or more."

"Well, I never!" exclaimed the astonished woman, staring at Robert as if she thought his mind was wandering. "What sort of business is it that's going to take so long?"

"The hermit wants it kept secret, Aunt Jane."

"But how am I going to get along without you?" asked his aunt in dismay. "I can't go out fishing, and the money I earn by sewing is almost nothing."

Robert smiled, for he knew he could allay his aunt's fears.

"The hermit will pay you five dollars a week while I am gone, and here is the first week's pay," he said, drawing from his pocket a bill.

"Well, I must say your friend the hermit is a gentleman. Five dollars a week is more than I can spend."

"Then save a part of it if you like, aunt."

"But what shall I do, Robert, if Mr. Jones comes upon me to pay the mortgage when you are gone?" said his aunt, with new alarm.

"The hermit has agreed to pay off the mortgage and take one himself for the same amount."

"He is very kind, Robert. Don't you think that I ought to call and thank him?"

"What! Call at the cave?"

"Yes!"

"No, aunt," said Robert hastily. "He would not like to have you. You can wait till you see him. But mind you don't tell anybody—least of all, Mr. Jones—that you will be able to pay the mortgage. As he is so mean, we want to give him a surprise."

"Just as you say, Robert. I am glad we'll be able to disappoint him, for he is certainly a very mean man. Now, when do you want to start for Boston?"

"To-morrow."

"But how am I going to get ready your shirts and socks so soon?"

"I shall not take any of them."

"Robert Coverdale, you must be crazy. You can't wear one shirt for two months if you're going so long."

"I don't expect to, aunt," said the boy, smiling. "I am going to buy a whole outfit of new things when I get to Boston. The hermit wants me to."

"He must be awful rich!" said the good woman, whose ideas on the subject of wealth were limited.

"All the better for us, Aunt Jane, as he is willing to spend some of his money for us."

Mrs. Trafton was considerably excited by the prospect of Robert's journey, and, notwithstanding what he had said, occupied herself in washing his clothes and making a small bundle for him to carry, but Robert declined taking them, with a smile.

"You see, aunt, my clothes wouldn't be good enough to wear in Boston," he said. "Just keep them till I get back. Perhaps I may need them then."

"I'll lay 'em away carefully, Robert. When you get a little larger I guess you'll be able to wear some of your uncle's clothes. His best suit might be made over for you. He hadn't had it but six years, and there's a good deal of wear in it yet. I might cut it over myself when you're gone."

"Better wait till I come back, aunt," said Robert hastily.

He knew the suit very well. It was snuff-colored and by no means a good fit, even for his uncle, while under his aunt's unpracticed hands it would probably look considerably worse when made over for him.

It must be confessed that Robert's ideas were expanding and he was rapidly growing more fastidious. He instinctively felt that he was about to turn a new leaf in his book of life and to enter on new scenes, in which he was to play a less obscure part than had been his hitherto in the little village of Cook's Harbor.

But no such change had come to his aunt. She still regarded Robert as the same boy that he always had been—born to the humble career of a fisherman—and she examined her husband's best suit with much complacency, mentally resolving that, in spite of Robert's objection, she would devote her leisure time to making it over for him.

"He can wear it for best for a year or two," she thought, "and then put it on every day. I am sure it will look well on him."

In the evening Robert went to the cave to have a farewell interview with the hermit—or Gilbert Huet, to give him the name which was properly his.

"You may write to me about once a week if you have anything to say, Robert," said the hermit.

"How shall I direct you, sir? Shall I use your name?"

"How am I known in the village?"

"They call you 'the hermit of the cliff.'"

"Then direct your letters to 'The Hermit of the Cliff.' They are not likely to go astray."

Mr. Huet gave Robert his instructions and finally produced a roll of banknotes.

"You will find two hundred dollars in this roll, Robert," he said. "You can buy a wallet to keep it in when you reach Boston."

"Two hundred dollars!" exclaimed the boy in amazement.

"You won't find it so large a sum as you suppose when you are required to pay traveling expenses. You need not try to be over-economical. I prefer that you should stop at good hotels and put on a good appearance. But I warn you to keep your mouth shut and tell your business to no one. I depend upon your discretion not to fall into the hands of knaves or adventurers. I know that I am putting unusual confidence in a boy of your limited experience, but I have no one else to trust, and I feel that you may be relied upon."

"I hope I shall not disappoint you, Mr. Huet."

"Well, Robert, I will bid you good night and God bless you! We don't know what lies before us, but if you succeed, I will take care that your career shall be a fortunate one."

Robert walked slowly back to his humble home, almost wishing that the night were over and his journey actually begun.

There was but one way out of Cook's Harbor—that is, by land. A stage left the village every morning for Kaneville, six miles distant, a small station on a road which terminated many miles away in Boston.

The stage started at seven o'clock, so Robert was forced to get up betimes, take an early breakfast and walk up to the tavern.

Mr. Jones, the landlord, was standing on the piazza when Robert made his appearance.

He had no proprietary right in the stage line, but the driver generally stopped overnight at the tavern and the horses were kept in his stable, so that he had come to assume a certain air of proprietorship.

As Robert was climbing up to take a seat by the driver Mr. Jones, with a frown, called out:

"Look here, you young rascal, come right down!"

"Why am I to come down, Mr. Jones?" said Robert independently.

"Because I tell you to. We can't have any boys stealing rides."

"Is this stage yours?" asked Robert, surveying the landlord with provoking coolness.

"No matter whether it is or not," retorted Jones, red in the face. "I tell you to come down. Do you hear?"

"Yes, I hear."

"Then you'd better come down double quick or I'll give you a taste of a horsewhip."

"I advise you to mind your own business, Mr. Jones," said Robert hotly, "and not interfere with the passengers by this stage."

"You're not a passenger, you young beggar!"

"I am a passenger—and now you'd better stop talking."

"Have you got money to pay your fare?" asked the landlord, beginning to suspect he had made a fool of himself.

"When the driver calls for the fare it will be time enough to tell."

"Luke," said Mr. Jones to the driver, "you'd better take that boy's fare now. He wants to swindle you out of a ride."

"You may take it out of this," said Robert, tendering a five-dollar bill.

"I guess we'll let it stand till we get to Kaneville," said Luke, gathering up the reins.

Robert darted a glance of triumph at the discomfited and bewildered landlord, and his journey was begun.

The latter, on Luke's return, learned to his further surprise that Robert had gone to Boston. On reflection, he concluded that Mrs. Trafton must have some relatives in the city from whom they hoped to borrow enough money to raise the mortgage.

"But he won't succeed, and in four weeks I shall turn him and his aunt out of doors," Mr. Jones complacently reflected.

CHAPTER XXIII
AN UNPLEASANT SURPRISE

When Robert arrived in Boston he was at first bewildered by the noise and bustle to which, in the quiet fishing village, he was quite unaccustomed. All that he knew about the city was the names of the principal streets.

It was not necessary, however, that he should go in any particular direction. He decided, therefore, to walk along, keeping a good lookout, and, when he saw a clothing store, to go in and provide a new outfit.

He was sensible that he was by no means dressed in city style. His clothes were coarse, and being cut and made by his aunt—who, though an excellent woman, was by no means an excellent tailor—looked countrified and outlandish.

The first hint Robert had of this was when two well-dressed boys, meeting him, simultaneously burst out laughing.

Robert was sensitive, but he was by no means bashful or timid. Accordingly he stepped up to the boys and demanded with kindling eyes:

"Are you laughing at me?"

"Oh, no, of course not," answered one of the boys, rolling his tongue in his cheek.

"Certainly not, my dear fellow," said the other, winking.

"I think you were," said Robert firmly. "Do you see anything to laugh at in me?"

"Well, to tell the truth," said the first boy, "we were wondering whether you import your clothes from Paris or London."

"Oh, that's it," said Robert good-humoredly, for he was aware that his clothes were of strange cut. "My clothes were made in the country and I don't think much of them myself. If you'd tell me where I can get some better ones I will buy a suit."

The boys were not bad-hearted and were won over by Robert's good humor.

"You're a good fellow," said the first speaker, "and I am sorry I was rude enough to laugh at you. There is a store where I think you can find what you want."

He pointed to a clothing store. In front of which was a good display of ready-made clothing.

"Thank you," said Robert.

He entered and the boys walked on.

If Robert had been better dressed he would have received immediate attention. As it was, he looked like a poor boy in want of work and not at all like a customer.

So, at all events, decided a dapper-looking clerk whose attention was drawn to the new arrival.

"Well, boy, what do you want?" he demanded roughly, approaching Robert.

"Civil treatment to begin with," answered Robert with spirit.

"If you've come for a place, we don't want any scarecrows here."

It appears that the firm had advertised for an errand boy that very morning, and it was naturally supposed that Robert was an applicant.

"Are you the owner of this shop?" asked Robert coolly.

"No," answered the clerk, lowering his tone a little.

"I thought so. I'll tell my business to somebody else."

"You'd better not put on airs!" said the clerk angrily.

"You are the one who is putting on airs," retorted Robert.

"What's the matter here?" asked a portly gentleman, walking up to the scene of the altercation.

"I was telling this boy that he would not do for the place," answered the clerk.

"I believe, Mr. Turner, that you are not commissioned to make a selection," said the gentleman.

And Turner retired, discomfited.

"So you want a place?" he said inquiringly to Robert.

"No, sir, I don't."

"Mr. Turner said you did."

"I never told him so."

"Here, Turner," said the gentleman. "Why did you tell me this boy wanted a place?"

"I supposed he did. He looked like it, sir."

"I don't want a place. I want to buy a suit of clothes," said Robert. "If that young man hadn't treated me so rudely, I should have asked him to show me some."

"Look here, Mr. Turner," said the gentleman sternly, "If you have no more sense than to insult our customers, we can dispense with your services. Mr. Conway, will you wait on this young man?"

Turner was mortified and slunk away, beginning to understand that it is not always safe to judge a man or boy by the clothes he wears.

Mr. Conway was more of a gentleman and civilly asked Robert to follow him.

"What kind of a suit would you like?" he added.

"A pretty good one," answered Robert.

He was shown several suits and finally selected one of gray mixed cloth of excellent quality.

"That is one of our most expensive suits," said Conway doubtfully.

"Will it wear well?"

"It will wear like iron."

"Then I will take it. How much will it cost?"

Conway named the price. Robert would have hesitated about paying so much, but that he was acting under instructions from the hermit.

"Shall we send it to you anywhere?" asked Mr. Conway, a little surprised at Robert's readiness to pay so high a price.

"No, I should like to put it on here."

"You can do so—that is, after paying for it."

Robert drew out a wallet and from his roll of bills took out sufficient to pay for the new suit.

47

Mr. Conway went to the cashier's desk. The two had a conversation together. Then the stout gentleman was called to the desk. Robert saw them open a copy of a morning paper and read a paragraph, looking at him after reading it. He wondered what it all meant.

Presently Conway came back and asked him to walk up to the desk.

Robert did so, wonderingly.

"You seem to have a good deal of money with you," commenced the stout gentleman.

"Yes, sir," answered Robert composedly.

"A great deal of money for a boy dressed as you are," continued the speaker pointedly.

Robert began to understand now, and he replied proudly:

"Do you generally ask your customers how much money they have?"

"No, but yours is a peculiar case."

"The money is mine—that is, I have a right to spend it. I am acting under orders from the gentleman who employs me."

"Who is that?"

"No one that you would know. He lives at Cook's Harbor. But I didn't come in here to answer questions. If you don't want to sell me a suit of clothes, I will go somewhere else."

"To be plain with you, my boy," said the stout gentleman, not unkindly, "we are afraid that you have no right to this money. The *Herald* of this morning gives an account of a boy who has run away from a town in New Hampshire with three hundred dollars belonging to a farmer. You appear to be the age mentioned."

"I never stole a dollar in my life," said Robert indignantly.

"It may be so, but I feel it a duty to put you in charge of the police, who will investigate the matter. James, call an officer."

Robert realized that he was in an unpleasant situation. It would be hard to prove that the money in his hands was really at his disposal.

Help came from an unexpected quarter.

A young man, fashionably dressed, had listened to the conversation of which Robert was the subject.

He came forward promptly, saying:

"There is no occasion to suspect this boy. He is all right."

"Do you know him?" asked the proprietor politely.

"Yes, I know him well. He is in the employ of a gentleman at Cook's Harbor, as he says. You can safely sell him the clothes."

The young man spoke so positively that all suspicion was removed.

"I am glad to learn that it is all right," said the clothing merchant. "My young friend, I am sorry to have suspected you. We shall be glad to sell you the suit, and to recompense you for the brief inconvenience we will take off two dollars from the price."

"Thank you, sir."

"It would not do for us to receive stolen money, hence our caution."

Robert did not bear malice, and he accepted the apology and dressed himself in the suit referred to, which very much changed his appearance for the better.

In fact, but for his hat and shoes, he looked like a city boy of a well-to-do family.

He felt fortunate in getting off so well, but he was puzzled to understand where he could have met the young man who professed to know him so well.

He left the store, but almost immediately was tapped on the shoulder by the young man in question.

"I got you off well, didn't I?" said the young man with a wink.

"I am much obliged to you, sir," said Robert.

"You don't seem to remember me," continued the young man, winking again.

"No, sir."

"Good reason why. I never saw you in my life before nor you me."

"But I thought you said you had met me at Cook's Harbor?" said Robert in surprise.

The young man laughed.

"Only way to get you off. You'd have been marched off by a policeman if I hadn't."

This seemed rather irregular to our hero. Still he knew that he was innocent of any wrongdoing, and as the young man appeared to have acted from friendly motives he thanked him again.

"That's all very well," said the young man, "but, considering the scrape I've saved you from, I think you ought to give me at least twenty-five dollars."

"But the money isn't mine," said Robert, opening his eyes, for he could hardly have expected an application for money from a young man so fashionably dressed.

48

"Of course it isn't," said the young man, winking again. "It belongs to the man you took it from. I'm fairly entitled to a part. So just give me twenty-five and we'll call it square."

"If you mean that I stole the money, you're quite mistaken," said Robert indignantly. "It belongs to my employer."

"Just what I thought," said the other.

"But I have a right to spend it. I am doing just as he told me to do."

"Come, young fellow, that won't go down! It's too thin!" said the young man, his countenance changing. "You don't take me in so easily. Just hand over twenty-five dollars or I'll hand you over to the police! There's one coming!"

Robert certainly did not care to have the threat executed, but he did not choose to yield.

"If you do," he said, "I'll tell him that you did it because I would not give you twenty-five dollars."

This did not strike his new acquaintance as desirable, since it would be, in effect, charging him with blackmail. Moreover, he could bring nothing tangible against our young hero. He changed his tone therefore.

"I don't want to harm you," he said, "but I deserve something for getting you out of a scrape. You might spare me five dollars."

"I got my suit two dollars cheaper through what you said," said Robert. "I'll give you that sum."

"Well, that will do," said the other, finding the country boy more unmanageable than he expected. "I ought to have more, but I will call it square on that."

Robert drew a two-dollar bill from his pocket and handed it to the stranger.

"That I can give," he said, "because it was part of the price of my suit."

"All right. Good morning!" said the young man, and, thrusting the bill into his vest pocket, he walked carelessly away.

Robert looked after him with a puzzled glance.

"I shouldn't think a young man dressed like that could be in want of money," he reflected. "I am afraid he told a lie on my account, but I thought at the time he had really seen me, even if I couldn't remember him."

Soon Robert came to a hat store, where he exchanged his battered old hat for one of fashionable shape, and a little later his cowhide shoes for a pair of neat calfskin. He surveyed himself now with natural satisfaction, for he was as well dressed as his friend Herbert Irving.

He had by this time reached Washington Street and had just passed Milk Street when he met George Randolph, who looked as consequential and conceited as ever.

"Good morning, George," said Robert.

George looked at him doubtfully.

How could he suppose that the boy before him, dressed as well as himself, was the poor fisher boy of Cook's Harbor?

"I don't seem to remember you," said George civilly.

Robert smiled.

"You met me at Cook's Harbor," he explained. "I am Robert Coverdale."

"What! not the young fisherman?" ejaculated George incredulously.

"The same."

"You haven't come into a fortune, have you? What brings you here?" demanded the city boy in great amazement.

"I am in the city on business. No, I haven't come into a fortune, but I am better off than I was. Can you recommend me a good hotel?"

"I don't know about the cheap hotels."

"I don't care for a cheap hotel. I want a good one."

More and more surprised, George said:

"You might go to Young's."

"I will go there. Thank you for telling me."

"I don't understand how a boy like you can afford to go to such a hotel as that," said George, looking very much puzzled.

"No, I suppose not," returned Robert, smiling.

"If you don't mind telling me——"

"I am sorry I can't, but my errand is a secret one."

"Did my uncle send you?"

"No, neither he nor Herbert knows of my coming. I didn't have time to see Herbert before I came away."

"Are you going to stay long in Boston?"

"No, I think not. I am going to New York or Albany."

49

"It seems queer to me."

"Very likely. Good-by! Thank you for directing me."

George had been remarkably civil, but in a boy like him that is easily explained. He was civil, not to Robert, but to his new suit and his new prosperity.

"It's the strangest thing I ever heard of," he muttered as he walked away. "Why, the young fisherman is dressed as well as I am!"

CHAPTER XXIV

ON LONG ISLAND SOUND

Had he possessed plenty of leisure, Robert would have been glad to remain in Boston long enough to see the principal objects of interest in the city and its vicinity, but he never for a moment forgot that his time was not his own.

He had entered the service of the hermit, and every day's delay was so much additional expense to his employer. True, Gilbert Huet was a rich man, as he had himself acknowledged, but Robert was conscientious, and felt that this would not justify him in gratifying himself at the expense of the man who had so trusted him.

Robert felt proud of this trust—this very unusual proof of confidence in a boy so young and inexperienced as he was—and he was ambitious to justify it. I am sure, therefore, that he would have had little satisfaction in postponing it out of regard to his own pleasure.

There were two ways of going to the West, which, it will be remembered, was his destination—by the way of Albany or New York City.

Finding that it would not matter much how he went, Robert decided upon the latter. It would enable him to see the great city of which he had heard so much, and who knows but, in this great metropolis, which swallows up so many, he might hear something of the lost boy?

He decided, therefore, to go at once to New York, and, after some inquiry, he fixed upon the Fall River route.

This includes railroad travel to Fall River, a distance of about fifty miles, where the traveler embarks on a great steamer and arrives in New York after a night on Long Island Sound.

Guided by an advertisement in the daily papers, Robert made his way to the Old State House, at the head of State Street, and, entering the office of the steamboat line, asked for a ticket.

"Will you take a stateroom also?" asked the clerk.

"Is that necessary?" asked Robert, who was unused to traveling.

"No, it's not necessary. Your ticket will entitle you to a comfortable berth, but in a stateroom you have greater privacy."

"What is a stateroom?" asked our hero.

The clerk was rather surprised by this question, but decided that Robert was not accustomed to traveling and answered politely enough:

"It is very much like a room in a hotel, only much smaller. There is a berth and a washstand, and you can lock yourself in. There is greater security against robbery, for you hold the key and no one can enter it without your knowledge."

As Robert carried considerable money belonging to Mr. Huet, he felt that he ought to take this precaution, if it were not too expensive.

"How much must I pay for a stateroom?" he asked.

"You can get a good one for a dollar."

"Then I will take one."

"Number fifty-six," said the clerk, handing him a card with the number penciled on it. "What's your name?"

"Robert Coverdale."

So Robert walked out of the office with his passage engaged.

This was on the morning after his arrival, and as the steamboat train did not start till afternoon, this afforded him a chance to spend several hours in seeing the city.

First he went to the Common and walked across it, surveying with interest the large and noble trees which add so much beauty to a park which, in size, is insignificant compared with the great parks of New York and Philadelphia, but appears older and more finished than either.

He rode in various directions in the cars and enjoyed the varied sights that passed under his notice.

At half-past four he paid his bill at the hotel and took a car which passed the depot from which the steamboat train for New York starts.

The train was an express, and in little more than an hour he boarded the beautiful Sound steamer.

He was astonished at its magnificence as he went upstairs to the main saloon. As he was looking about him in rather a bewildered way a colored man employed on the boat inquired:

"What are you looking for, young man?"

"Where shall I get a key to my stateroom?"

He was told, and, opening the door, he found himself in a comfortable little room with two berths.

"I can pass the night here very pleasantly," he thought. "There is some difference between sleeping here and on a sailboat."

Once, in company with his uncle, he had been compelled to pass the night on the ocean in a small sailboat used for fishing purposes.

Robert left his valise in the stateroom and went into the saloon.

A gong was heard, which he found was the announcement of supper. It was now past seven o'clock and he felt hungry. He accordingly followed the crowd downstairs and ate a hearty meal.

When he went upstairs again the band soon began to play and helped to while away the time. Some of the passengers read papers, others read books and magazines, while others from the outer decks watched the progress of the large boat as it swiftly coursed over the waves. In this last company was Robert.

Without being aware of it, our hero attracted the notice of one of his fellow passengers, a man possibly of thirty-five, tall and thin and dressed in black. Finally he accosted Robert.

"A fine evening!" he remarked.

"Yes, sir, very fine."

"You are going to New York, I suppose?"

"Yes, sir."

"Do you tarry there?"

"Not long. I am going to Ohio."

"You seem young to travel alone. Perhaps, however, you have company?"

"No, sir," Robert answered. "I am traveling alone."

There was a look of satisfaction on the man's face, which Robert did not see. Even if he had he would not have known how to interpret it.

"It is pleasant to go to New York by boat," said the stranger. "I prefer it to the cars; that is, when I can get a stateroom. Did you secure one?"

"Yes, sir."

"You are more fortunate than I. I found they had all been taken. I would not care so much if I were not suffering from fever and ague."

"I suppose you have a berth?" said Robert.

"Yes, but the berths are exposed to draughts and are not as desirable as staterooms."

Robert did not know that, so far from this being the case, the great fault of the ordinary berths was a lack of air.

"I suppose your stateroom contains two berths?" said the stranger.

"Yes, I believe so."

"I may be taking a liberty, but I have a proposal to make. If you will allow me to occupy one of them I will pay half the cost of your room. It would oblige me very much, but I would not ask if I were not sick."

Robert did not entirely like this proposal. He preferred to be alone. Still he was naturally obliging, and he hardly knew how to refuse this favor to a sick man.

"I see you hesitate," said the stranger. "Pray think no more of my request. I would not mind paying the entire cost of the room, if you will take me in. It cost you a dollar, did it not?"

"Yes, sir."

"Then," said the man, drawing a dollar bill from his pocketbook, "allow me to pay for it and share it with you."

"I ought not to be selfish," thought Robert. "I would rather be alone, but if this man is sick I think I will let him come in with me."

He so expressed himself, and the other thanked him warmly and pressed the dollar upon him.

"No," said Robert, "I can't take so much. You may pay for your share—fifty cents."

"You are very kind," murmured the other.

And, replacing the bill in his pocketbook, he took out a half dollar and tendered it to our hero.

Half an hour later both repaired to stateroom No. 56.

As they entered the room the stranger glanced at the two berths and said:

"It is only fair that you should occupy the best berth."

"Which is the best berth?" asked Robert.

"The lower one is generally so considered," said the other. "It is a little wider and it is less trouble to get into it. I will take the upper one."

"No," said Robert generously. "You are sick and ought to have the best. I am perfectly well, and I shan't mind climbing into the upper one."

"But it seems so selfish in me," protested the stranger, "to step into your stateroom and take the best accommodations."

"Not if I am willing," responded Robert cheerfully. "So it is all settled."

"How kind you are!" murmured the invalid. "Though we have met so recently, I cannot help feeling toward you as if you were my younger brother."

Robert thanked him, but could hardly reciprocate the feeling. In truth, he had taken no fancy to the man whom he had accepted as roommate and was only influenced by compassion for his reported sickness.

They undressed and retired to their berths. As the stranger was about to step into his he said:

"It is only fair to tell you my name. I am called Mortimer Fairfax and I am a partner in a business firm in Baltimore. Are you in business?"

"Not exactly," answered Robert, "though I am traveling on business just now."

"I believe you didn't mention your name," said Fairfax.

"My name is Robert Coverdale."

"An excellent name. I know a family in Philadelphia by that name. Are you sleepy?"

"A little."

"Then suppose we go to sleep?"

"All right. Goodnight!"

Then there was silence in the stateroom.

It was not long before Robert's eyes closed. He had gone about considerable during the day and was naturally fatigued. Generally he had no difficulty in sleeping soundly, but to-night proved an exception. He tossed about in his narrow berth and he was troubled with disagreeable dreams. Sometimes it happens that such dreams visit us to warn us of impending danger.

Robert finally dreamed that a pickpocket had drawn his pocketbook from his pocket and was running away with it, and he awoke with a sudden start, his face bathed in perspiration.

It was midnight. The band had ceased playing for two hours and all who had staterooms had retired to them. Only here and there in the main saloon a passenger lay asleep in an armchair.

There was a scanty light, which entered the stateroom through a small window, and by this light Robert, half rising in bed, saw a sight that startled him.

Mr. Mortimer Fairfax, his roommate, was out of his berth. He had taken down Robert's trousers from the nail on which he had hung them and was in the act of pulling out his wallet, which he had imprudently left in it.

This sight fully aroused the lad, and he prepared for action.

Fairfax was half bent over, and Robert, who was deeply incensed, threw himself from the upper berth, landing on the back of his roommate, who was borne to the floor, releasing the garment with a startled cry.

"What did you do that for?" he asked nervously.

"What business had you with my pocketbook, you thief?" demanded Robert sternly.

Mortimer Fairfax, who had supposed Robert to be fast asleep, saw that he was in a scrape, but he was a man fertile in expedients, and he instantly decided upon his course.

"What do you mean?" he inquired in a tone of innocent bewilderment.

"What do I mean?" retorted our hero. "I want to know what business you had with my pocketbook in your hand?"

"You don't mean to say that I was meddling with your pocketbook?" said Fairfax with an air of surprise.

"That is exactly what I do say, Mr. Fairfax. If I hadn't waked up just as I did, you would have had all my money, and I should have been penniless. That is the sort of fever and ague that troubles you, I suppose."

"My young friend," said Fairfax, "I am shocked at what you tell me. I do not blame you for accusing me. If I were in your place and you in mine, I should no doubt act in the same way. Yet I am entirely innocent, I can assure you."

"It don't look much like it," Robert said, rather astonished at the man's effrontery. "When I find you examining my pockets and taking out my pocketbook, it looks very much as if you were trying to rob me."

"True, it does. I admit it all. But if you knew me, you would see how groundless, nay, how absurd such suspicions are. Why, I am a rich man. I am worth fifty thousand dollars."

"Then why did you try to rob me?"

"I did not. It was only in appearance. Did you ever hear of a somnambulist?"

"No."

"It is one who gets up in his sleep and is entirely unconscious of what he does. From early youth—from the days of my innocent boyhood—I have been a victim of this unfortunate malady."

"Do you often steal in your sleep?" inquired Robert sarcastically.

"Not often, but I have done it before. Once, when a boy, I got up and took a purse from the pocket of my uncle, who occupied the same room with me."

"What did your uncle say?" Robert asked with some curiosity.

"He was angry till my mother assured him that I was a somnambulist and not responsible for what I did at such a time. Then we had a good laugh, over it."

"Do you mean to say, Mr. Fairfax, that when you had your hand in my pocket just now you were asleep?"

"Sound asleep. I had no idea that I was out of my berth."

"You seemed to wake up pretty quick afterward!"

"To be sure I did! I rather think you would wake up, too, if I should jump upon your back from the top berth! But I forgive you—don't apologize, I beg. I should have been misled, as you were, if our situations had been changed."

Certainly Mr. Mortimer Fairfax was cool.

In his limited acquaintance with the world Robert had never dreamed of the existence of such a character, but he was gifted with shrewd common sense, and he did not for an instant believe the story which the other palmed off upon him.

"Mr. Fairfax," he said, "shall I tell you what I think of your story?"

"Yes, if you please."

"I don't believe it."

"What!" exclaimed Fairfax sadly. "Is it possible you believe that I would rob you, my kind benefactor?"

"I don't pretend to be your benefactor, but I haven't a doubt about it."

"My dear young friend," said Fairfax, putting his handkerchief to his eyes, "you grieve me deeply—indeed you do! I had thought you would understand me better. You do not consider that I am a rich man and can have no object in depriving you of your little store of money. Let us go to bed and forget this unpleasant little circumstance."

"No, Mr. Fairfax, you cannot stay here any longer. I insist upon your dressing yourself and leaving the stateroom!"

"But, my young friend. It is the middle of the night!"

"I can't help it!" said Robert resolutely.

"And, in my delicate health, it would be dangerous."

"I don't believe you are in delicate health, but I can't help it if you are. You must go!"

"You forget," said Fairfax in a different tone, "that half of the stateroom is mine. I have paid for it."

"Then I will return the money. Here it is."

"I prefer to remain here."

"If you don't go," said Robert energetically, "I will call for help and report that you tried to rob me!"

"You will repent this unkind treatment," said Fairfax sullenly, but he proceeded to dress nevertheless, and in a few minutes he left the stateroom.

Robert locked the door after him and then, returning to bed, he said with a sigh of relief:

"Now I can sleep without fear. I am sure that fellow is a rascal, and I am glad to be rid of him."

CHAPTER XXV

A BAGGAGE SMASHER'S REVENGE

When Robert awoke in the morning it was eight o'clock and the steamer lay quietly at its pier. Almost all the passengers had landed and he was nearly alone on the great steamer.

Of course Mortimer Fairfax had gone with the rest; in fact, Fairfax was one of the first to land. He had passed the remainder of the night in the saloon, anxious, as long as he remained on board, lest Robert should denounce him for his attempted theft.

Robert was a stranger in New York. He was instantly impressed by what he could see of the great city from the deck of the steamer. He took his valise In his hand and walked across the gangplank upon the pier. At the entrance he was accosted by a hackman.

"Carriage, sir?"

"No," answered Robert.

"I will carry you cheap."

"What do you call cheap?"
"Where do you want to go?"
"Astor House."
This hotel had been suggested by the hermit.
"All right! Jump in!" and the hackman was about to take Robert's valise.
"Wait a moment," said the lad firmly. "I haven't agreed to ride. What do you charge?"
"Two dollars."
"Two dollars! How far is it?"
"About five miles!" answered the hackman with unblushing falsehood.
"Is there no stage that goes to that part of the city?"
"No; your only way is to take a carriage."
Though Robert had never before been in New York, he felt convinced that this was untrue and said quietly:
"Then I will walk."
"It is too far, young man. Nobody walks up there."
"Then I'll be the first one to try it!" said Robert coolly.
"Wait a minute, youngster! I'll take you for a dollar and a half."
Robert did not answer, but crossed the street.
"Carry your bag, sir?" said a boy of about his own age, who seemed to be waiting for a job.
"Do you know the way to the Astor House?" asked Robert.
"I ought to."
"How far is it?"
"Half a mile."
"That hack driver told me it was five miles."
The boy grinned.
"He thought you were green," he said. "Say, boss, shall I carry that v'lise?"
"How much do you charge?"
"I'll take it to Broadway for a quarter."
"All right. I'll pay it."
"I see," thought Robert, "I shall have to look out or I shall be cheated. It seems to cost a good deal of money to travel."
As Robert walked along he asked various questions of his young partner as to the buildings which they passed. On reaching Broadway he said:
"I don't care about riding. If you will walk along with me and carry the valise I will pay you a quarter more."
"All right. Only pay me the first quarter now," said the boy cautiously.
"Just as you like. Are you afraid I won't pay you."
"I dunno. I was served that way once."
"How was it?"
"I was carryin' a bag—a thunderin' big bag it was, too—for a man to this very hotel. I'd carried it about a mile; when we got there he took it and was goin' in without payin' me.
"'Look here, boss,' I says, 'you haven't paid me.'
"'Yes, I did,' he says. 'I paid you when you took the bag.'
"Then I knew he was a beat, and I made a fuss, I tell you, and follered him into the hotel.
"'What's the matter?' asked one of the hotel men, comin' forrard.
"'This boy wants me to pay him twice,' he says.
"Of course, the hotel people took up for the man and kicked me out of the hotel. I didn't blame them so much, for who'd think of a gentleman cheatin' a poor boy?"
"That was pretty hard on you," said Robert in a tone of sympathy. "He must have been a mean man."
"Mean? I guess he was. But I got even with him, and I didn't wait long neither."
"How was that?"
"I got an egg and I laid for him. Toward night he come out, all dressed up like as if he was goin' to the theayter. I follered him, and when I got a good chance I just hove it at him. I hit him just in his bosom, and the egg was spattered over his face and clothes. He gave a yell and then I dodged round the corner. Oh, it was rich to see how he looked! I guess he'd better have paid me."
Robert could not help laughing, and did not find it in his heart to blame the boy who had chosen this summary way to redress his grievances.
"I hope," he said, "you haven't got any eggs with you now."
"Why, ain't you goin' to pay me?"
"Oh, yes, I mean to pay you. I wouldn't cheat a poor boy. I'm a poor boy myself."

54

His guide looked at him in surprise.

"You a poor boy, with them clo'es?" he repeated. "If you was a poor boy you wouldn't pay me for carryin' your baggage."

"But would carry it myself?"

"Yes."

"So I would, but I wanted somebody to guide me to the hotel. I am traveling for a gentleman that pays the bills."

"Oh, cricky! ain't that jolly? Wouldn't he like me to travel for him?"

"I guess not," said Robert, laughing.

"If he should, just give a feller a chance."

"I might, if I knew your name and where you live."

"I left my cardcase at home on the planner, along with my jewelry, but my name's Michael Burke. The boys call me Mike. I live at the Newsboys' Lodge, when I'm at home."

"All right, Mike; I'll remember."

The remainder of the walk was enlivened by conversation of a similar kind. Though Mike was not much of a scholar, he was well informed on local matters, and it was upon such points that Robert wished to be posted.

When they reached the hotel Mike uttered an exclamation of surprise.

"Say, do you see that man in the doorway?" he asked eagerly.

"What of him?"

"He's the very man that cheated me out of my pay—the man I hit wid an egg. Here he is again."

Robert surveyed the man with curious interest. He was a man of middle age, well dressed, but with a hard, stern look upon his face. He was by no means one likely to attract strangers.

"How do you know it is the same one?" asked Robert in a low voice.

"He's got the same look. I'd remember him if it was a dozen years, but it's only six months."

"But you might be mistaken."

"I'll show you whether I am. Come along."

When they entered the vestibule of the hotel Mike paused a moment and, in hearing of the stranger, said:

"Last night, as I was walkin' along, I seed a man hit wid a rotten egg. He looked mad enough to kill the one that throwed it."

The stranger wheeled round and regarded Mike intently.

"Boy," said he, "I think I've seen you before."

"Maybe you have," answered Mike coolly. "Lots of people has seen me."

"Did you ever carry a valise for me?"

"Maybe I did. I've carried lots of 'em."

"I think you once brought a valise for me to this very hotel."

"How much did you pay me for doin' it? Maybe I could tell by that."

"I don't know. I presume I paid you liberally."

"Then I guess it was some other boy," said Mike, grinning.

The gentleman looked puzzled, but just then a young man came up and spoke to him, addressing him as "Mr. Waldo."

Robert started at the sound of this name. He remembered that this was the name of his employer's cousin, who was suspected of abducting the boy of whom he was in search.

Bidding good-by to his young guide, he registered his name and then turned over the pages back. In the list of arrivals for the day before he came upon this entry:

"Charles Waldo, Sullivan, Ohio."

"It's the very man!" he said to himself in excitement.

CHAPTER XXVI
TWO IMPORTANT DISCOVERIES

Charles Waldo was the name of the hermit's cousin, who was suspected of kidnapping the boy who stood between him and the property. It was to find this very man that Robert was sent out by Gilbert Huet.

Robert felt that he was fortunate in so soon running across this man and decided that as long as Mr. Waldo remained in the hotel it was his policy to remain also.

He did not see how he was to find out anything about the missing boy, but resolved to watch and wait in the hope of obtaining a clew. He did not wish to attract Mr. Waldo's suspicions, but took care to keep him in view.

55

The next morning he observed Mr. Waldo in the reading room at the rear of the hotel talking with another person—rather a pretentious-looking man, with black whiskers and a jaunty air.

At the news stand he bought a copy of a morning paper and took a seat sufficiently near to hear what was said.

Though Waldo and his companion spoke in low tones, neither was apprehensive of being heard, as it was hardly to be presumed that any one within hearing distance would feel an interest in what they had to say.

"As I was saying"—this was the first sentence which Robert heard from Mr. Waldo—"it is entirely uncertain when I shall derive any advantage from my cousin's estate. During his life he holds it."

"How is his health?"

"I suppose he is well. In fact, I don't know but he is likely to live as long as I do. There can't be more than five years' difference in our ages."

"That is a discouraging outlook."

"I should say so! But there is one chance for me during his life."

"What is that?"

"He may be declared insane. In that case the management of the estate would naturally be transferred to me as the direct heir."

"But is there any ground for assumption that he is insane?"

"Yes. Ever since his son's death he has acted in an eccentric way—made a hermit of himself and withdrawn from society. You know grief brooded over often terminates in insanity. Then there was his wife's terrible death, which had a strange effect upon him."

"I did not understand that the boy died."

"Well, he disappeared. He is undoubtedly dead."

"It is his being out of the way that makes you the heir, is it not?"

"Of course," answered Waldo.

"Then all I can say is that it was mighty fortunate for you," said his companion dryly.

"It hasn't done me any good yet and may not. These hermits are likely to live long. Their habits are regular and they are not tempted to violate the laws of health. I tell you, Mr. Thompson, it's a tantalizing thing to be so near a large fortune and yet kept out of it."

"I suppose you pray for your cousin's death, then?"

"Not so bad as that, but, as he don't enjoy the property, it is a pity I can't."

"How much does the estate amount to probably?" asked the other with interest.

"Well, it can't be less than two hundred thousand dollars."

"Whew! That's a great fortune!"

"So it is. If I get it, or when I get it, I won't mind doing as you ask me, and setting you up in a snug business."

"You could do it now, Mr. Waldo. You are a rich man," said Thompson.

"You are mistaken. I may have a competence, but nothing more."

"You've got a fine farm."

"That don't support me. Farming doesn't pay."

"And money in stock and bonds."

"Enough to make up the deficiency in my income. I assure you I don't lay up a cent. I can't do it."

"May I ask what is your errand in New York?"

"I want to speak to you about that. I want to find my cousin."

"Don't his bankers know where he is?"

"If they do, they won't tell. I suppose they are acting under orders from him?"

"Suppose you find him?"

"Then," said Charles Waldo significantly, "I shall raise the question of his sanity. It won't be a difficult matter to prove him insane. It only needs a certificate from a couple of doctors. I think I can find two parties who will oblige me."

"I say, Waldo, you're a cool, calculating fellow!" Thompson was about to use another word, but checked himself. "I wouldn't like to stand in your way."

"Nonsense! I only want to do what is right."

"And it very conveniently happens that you consider right what is to your interest. I say, have you any idea how the boy came to disappear?"

"Of course not! How should I?" answered Waldo uneasily.

"I don't know, but as he stood in your way, I thought——"

"You think too much," said Waldo.

"Oh, I don't mean to censure you. I suppose if I had been in your place I might have been tempted."

"I know nothing about the boy's disappearance," said Waldo hastily; "but let us drop that. I sent for you because I saw that you could serve me."

"Go on; if there's money in it, I am your man."

"I shall pay you, of course; that is, I will pay you fairly. We will speak of that hereafter."

"What do you want me to do? Is there anybody you want to disappear?"

"Hush! You go too far, sir. I want to find out the whereabouts of Gilbert Huet. It is important for me to know where he is."

"Can you give me a clew?"

"If I could I should not need to employ you. Come up to my room and I will communicate further with you."

The two left the reading room and Robert was left to digest the important information he had received.

"What a rascal that man is!" he reflected. "After stealing Mr. Huet's boy, he wants to put him in a madhouse. I must let him know, so that he may be on his guard. I don't believe they will think of looking for him at Cook's Harbor."

By a curious coincidence the room assigned to Robert was next to that occupied by Mr. Waldo, and when the boy was about entering it, some hours later, he saw the gentleman going in just ahead of him.

As the latter placed one hand upon the door he drew his handkerchief from his coat pocket, and in so doing brought out a letter, which fell upon the floor, without his seeing it.

Passing into his room, he slammed the door, leaving the missive lying in the hall.

"It is a mean thing," laughed Robert as he stooped down and picked it up, "to examine a letter not intended for me, but he is such a scamp that I'll do it in this case, hoping to learn something that will help me find this poor boy."

And so, without any compunctions, Robert took the letter—which had been opened—into his room and read, with feelings which may possibly be imagined, the following letter:

"DEAR SIR: I feel obligded to rite to you about the boy I took from you. You told me he would work enough to pay for his keep, and did not want to pay me anything for my trubble. Now, Mr. Waldo, you are mistaken. The boy ain't tuff nor strong, and I can't got more'n half as much work out of him as I ought. He don't eat much, I kno, but the fact is I need a good strong boy, and I shall have to git another, and have two to feed, if things go on so.

"You told me I might be strict and harsh with him, and I am. He says he has the headache about half the time, but I don't pay no attenshun to that. If I did, I wouldn't git any work done. One day he fainted away in the feald, but it's my opinyun he brought it on a-purpose by not eatin' much breakfast.

"I tell you, Mr. Waldo, it is very aggravatin' to have such a shifless boy. Now, what I want to ask you is, if you can't allow me a dollar, or a dollar and a half a week to make it square. I'm willin' to take care of the boy, but I don't want to lose money by it. I kno you give him his clo'es, but that don't cost you much. He ain't had a suit for a year, and he needs one bad.

"I'm sure you will see the thing the way I do, if you are a reasonable man, as I have no reason to doubt you are; and so I remain yours to command, NATHAN BADGER.

"To MR. CHARLES WALDO."

Robert could hardly express his excitement and indignation when he was reading this letter. He felt sure that this poor boy, who was so cruelly treated, was the unfortunate son of his friend, the hermit, who ought to be enjoying the comforts of a luxurious home. As it was, he was the victim of a cruel and unscrupulous relative, influenced by the most mercenary motives.

"I will be his friend," Robert resolved, "and if I can I will restore him to his father."

He looked for the date of the letter and found it. It had been written in the town of Dexter, in Ohio. Where this town was Robert did not know, but he could find out.

"I won't wait for Mr. Waldo," he said to himself. "I know all I need to. I will start for Ohio to-morrow."

As for the letter, he resolved to keep it, as it might turn out to be important evidence in case of need.

He could not understand how Mr. Waldo could be careless enough to mislay so important a document, but this did not concern him. It was his business to profit by it.

CHAPTER XXVII
THE BOUND BOY

The town of Dexter was almost entirely agricultural. Its population was small and scattered. There were no large shops or manufactories to draw people to the place. Many of the farmers were well to do, carrying on agricultural operations on a considerable scale.

Among the smaller farmers was Nathan Badger. He was fond of money, but knew no better way to get it than to live meanly, drive hard bargains and spend as little as possible. In this way, though not a very good farmer, he was able to lay by a couple of hundred dollars a year, which he put away in the County Savings Bank.

Mrs. Badger was a fitting wife for such a man. She was about as mean as he was, with scarcely any of the traits that make women attractive. She had one, however—an indulgent love of her only child, Andrew Jackson Badger, who was about as disagreeable a cub as can well be imagined. Yet I am not sure that Andrew was wholly responsible for his ugliness, as most of his bad traits came to him by inheritance from the admirable pair whom he called father and mother.

Andrew Jackson Badger was by no means a youthful Apollo. To speak more plainly, he was no beauty. A tow head and freckled face often belong to a prepossessing boy of popular manners, but in Andrew's case they were joined to insignificant features, small ferret eyes, a retreating chin and thin lips, set off by a repulsive expression.

There was another member of the family—a bound boy—the same one referred to in Mr. Nathan Badger's letter. This boy was, five years previous, placed in Mr. Badger's charge by Charles Waldo.

I do not want my young readers to remain under any uncertainty as to this boy, and I state at once that he was the abducted son of Gilbert Huet, the hermit of Cook's Harbor, and the rightful heir to a large estate.

At the time of our introduction to Bill Benton—for this is the name by which he was known—he had a hoe in his hand and he was about starting for the field to hoe potatoes.

He was a slender boy, with delicate features and a face which indicated a sensitive temperament. His hair was dark brown, his features were refined, his eyes were blue and he looked like a boy of affectionate temperament, who would feel injustice and harshness keenly. This was indeed the case. He lacked the strong, sturdy character, the energy and self-reliance which made Robert Coverdale successful. Robert was not a boy to submit to injustice or wrong. He was not easily intimidated and could resist imposition with all his might. But Bill—to call him by the name given him by Mr. Waldo—was of a more gentle, yielding disposition, and so he was doomed to suffer.

He was certainly unfortunately situated. Mr. Badger required him to work beyond his strength and seldom, or never, gave him a kind word. The same may be said of Mrs. Badger. It was perhaps fortunate for him that he had a small appetite, for in the Badger household he would have been unable to gratify the hearty appetite of an average boy.

The table was very mean and the only one who lived well was Andrew Jackson, whom his mother petted and indulged. There was always something extra on the table for Andrew, which it was well understood that no one else in the family was to eat.

Mr. Badger did not interfere with his wife's petting. If he had a soft place in his heart, it was for Andrew, who seemed to his partial parents a remarkably smart and interesting boy.

To Bill Benton he was a cruel tyrant. He delighted in making the life of his father's bound boy intolerable, and succeeded only too well. He was stronger than Bill, and, backed by the authority of his father and mother, he dared do anything, while Bill knew that it was useless to resist. Still, gentle as he was, sometimes his spirit rose and made a feeble resistance.

"Where are you going, Bill?" asked Andrew as the bound boy started off after breakfast.

"I am going to hoe potatoes, Andrew."

"No, you're not; I want you to go and dig some worms for bait. I am going a-fishing."

"But your father told me to go to the field at once."

"I can't help that. He didn't know I wanted you."

"He will scold me if I don't go to work."

"That is my business. I tell you to go and dig some worms."

Poor Bill! He knew very well that if Andrew got him into a scrape, he would not help him out, but leave his father to suppose that Bill disobeyed of his own accord—if necessary, stoutly asserting it, for Andrew was by no means a boy of truth.

"I would rather not go, Andrew," said Bill uneasily.

"Then take that!"

And Andrew brutally struck him with a whip he had in his hand.

The bound boy flushed at this indignity. Gentle as he was, he resented a blow.

"Don't you do that again, Andrew!" he said. "I won't stand it!"

"You won't stand it?" repeated Andrew tauntingly. "What will you do about it, I'd like to know?"

"You have no right to hit me, and I won't submit to it," said Bill with a spirit which quite astonished the young tyrant.

He laughed scornfully and repeated the blow, but with more emphasis.

Even the most gentle and long-suffering turn sometimes, and this was the case now.

The bound boy lifted the hoe and with the handle struck Andrew so forcibly that he dropped upon the ground, bellowing like a calf.

Like most bullies he was cowardly, and the unexpected resistance and the pain of the blow quite overcame his fortitude, and he cried like a baby.

It must be confessed that the bound boy was frightened by what he had done. Too well he knew that he would suffer for his temerity. Besides, his compassion was aroused for Andrew, whom he thought to be worse hurt than he was.

He threw down the hoe and kneeled by the prostrate boy.

"Oh, Andrew, I hope I didn't hurt you!" he cried. "I ought not to have struck you."

"You'll catch it when father comes home!" screamed Andrew furiously. "You almost killed me!"

"Oh, Andrew, I'm so sorry. I hope you'll forgive me."

By this time Mrs. Badger had come to the door, and Andrew, catching a glimpse of her, gave a yell as if in extreme anguish.

His mother came flying out of the house.

"What's the matter, my darling?" she cried in alarm.

"Bill knocked me down with a hoe, and I think I'm going to die!" answered Andrew with a fresh burst of anguish.

Mrs. Badger was almost paralyzed with astonishment and wrath. She could hardly believe her ears. What! Her Andrew assaulted by a beggarly bound boy!

"Bill knocked you down with a hoe?" she repeated. "You don't mean it?"

"Yes, I do. Ask him if he didn't."

"Bill Benton," said Mrs. Badger in an awful voice, "did you strike Andrew with a hoe?"

"Yes, ma'am, and I'm sorry for it, but he struck me with a whip first."

"No doubt he had a good reason for doing it. And so you tried to murder him, you young ruffian?"

"No, I didn't, Mrs. Badger. He had no right to whip me, and I defended myself. But I'm sorry——"

Andrew set up another howl, though he no longer felt any pain, and his mother's wrath increased.

"You'll end your life on the gallows, you young brute!" she exclaimed, glaring wrathfully at the poor boy. "Some night you'll try to murder us all in our beds. The only place for you is in jail! When Mr. Badger comes home, I will report the case to him. Now, go to work."

Poor Bill was glad to get away from the infuriated woman.

Andrew was taken into the house and fed on preserves and sweetmeats by his doting mother, while the poor bound boy was toiling in the hot sun, dreading the return of his stern master.

Nathan Badger was not far away. He had driven to the village in the buggy, not that he had any particular business there, but at present there was no farm work of a pressing nature except what the bound boy could do, and Mr. Badger did not love work for its own sake.

In spite of his parsimony, he generally indulged himself in a glass of bitters, of which he was very fond, whenever he went to the village. His parsimony stood him in good stead in one respect, at least, for it prevented his becoming a drunkard.

I have said that Mr. Badger had no particular business at the village, but this is not strictly true. He had business at the post office.

Some time since he had written to Mr. Waldo, asking for a money allowance for the care of Bill Benton. He knew very well that he was not entitled to it. He was at no expense for the boy's clothes, and certainly Bill richly earned the very frugal fare, of which he partook sparingly, and the privilege of a hard bed in the attic. But it had struck him as possible that Mr. Waldo, not knowing the falsehood of his representations, would comply with his request.

"If I can get a dollar or a dollar 'n' a half for the boy's keep," Mr. Badger soliloquized, "I can make a good thing out'n him. A dollar a week will come to fifty-two dollars a year, and I can't put a cent into the savings bank. A dollar 'n' a half will come to—lemme see—to seventy-eight dollars a year! That, in five years, would be three hundred and ninety dollars, without counting the interest."

Mr. Badger's eyes glistened and his heart was elated as he took in the magnificent idea.

But, alas! he was counting chickens that were not likely to be hatched.

When sufficient time had elapsed for an answer to be due, he went to the post office every day, but there had been unusual delay. At last an answer had been received that very morning.

Mr. Badger tore open the envelope in eager haste, but there was no remittance, as he had fondly hoped. The contents of the letter also threw cold water on his aspiring hopes, as may be seen from the following transcript of it:

"MR. NATHAN BADGER: Your letter is received asking me to pay you a weekly sum for the boy whom I bound out to you some years ago. I can hardly express the surprise I felt at this application. You certainly cannot forget that I furnish the boy's clothes, and that all you are required to do is to provide him board and lodging in return for his work. This is certainly a very good bargain for you. I need not say that the work of a boy of fifteen or sixteen years will amply repay you for his board, especially if, as I infer from your letter, he is a small eater. Generally farmers are willing to provide clothes also, and I think I am dealing very liberally with you in exempting you from this additional expense.

"You seem to forget one thing more: For three years, on account of the boy's being young, and so unable to work much, I allowed you fifty dollars a year, though I could readily have found another man to take him without this allowance. Under the circumstances I consider it very extraordinary that you should apply to me at this late day for an extra allowance. I am not made of money, and whatever I do for this boy is out of pure benevolence, for he has no claim upon me; but I assure you that I will not be imposed upon, therefore I say 'no' most emphatically.

"One other thing. You say the boy doesn't work as much as he ought to. I can only say this is no business of mine. You have full authority over him, and you can make him work. I don't believe in pampering boys and indulging them in laziness. I recommend you to be strict with William—to let him understand that you are not to be trifled with. Such would be my course. Yours, etc.,

"CHARLES WALDO."

Nathan Badger was deeply disappointed. He had made up his mind that Mr. Waldo would allow him at least a dollar a week and had complacently calculated how much this would enable him to lay aside. Now this dream was over.

Of course he could have given up the boy, for he was not formally bound to him. But this he did not care to do. The fact was that Bill earned his board twice over, and Mr. Badger knew it, though he would not have admitted it. It was for his interest to keep him.

He went home deeply disappointed and angry and disposed to vent his spite on the poor victim of his tyranny, even had there been no plausible excuse for doing so.

When he reached home he was met by Mrs. Badger with a frowning brow.

"Well, Mr. Badger, there's been a pretty scene since you went away."

"What do you mean, Cornelia?"

"Bill has nearly killed Andrew Jackson."

"Are you crazy, wife?"

"No, I am in earnest. The young rascal attacked poor Andrew with a hoe and nearly killed him."

"Then he must be crazy!" ejaculated Mr. Badger. "Where is Andrew? I want his account of it. If it is as you say, the boy shall suffer."

CHAPTER XXVIII
THE VICTIM OF TYRANNY

Andrew Jackson made his appearance with a piece of brown paper over an imaginary bruise on his head and eye and the carefully assumed expression of a suffering victim.

"What is this I hear?" asked his father. "Have you had a difficulty with Bill?"

"Yes," answered Andrew in the tone of a martyr. "He knocked me down with a hoe, and if mother had not come out just as she did I think he would have killed me."

"What made him attack you?" asked Mr. Badger, exceedingly surprised.

"I asked him if he would dig some fish-worms for me."

"Couldn't you dig some yourself?"

"I s'pose I could, but he knew better than I where to find them."

"What next?"

"He said he wouldn't. I told him that I would tell you about his impertinence. Then he hit me with the hoe as hard as he could."

"Was that all that passed?"

"Yes."

"I don't quite understand it. You are surely stronger than Bill. How did it happen that you allowed him to strike you?"

"He had a hoe and I hadn't anything," answered Andrew meekly. "He was so furious that he wouldn't have made anything of killing me."

"I always thought he was rather mild and milk-and-watery," said Nathan Badger thoughtfully.

"You wouldn't have thought so if you'd seen him, Mr. Badger," said his wife, drawing upon her imagination. "He looked like a young fiend. Dear Andrew is right. The boy is positively dangerous! I don't know but we shall be murdered in our beds some night if we let him go on this way."

Mr. Badger shrugged his shoulders, for he was not quite a fool, and answered dryly: "That thought won't keep me awake. He isn't that kind of a boy."

"Oh, well, Mr. Badger, if you are going to take his part against your own flesh and blood, I've got no more to say."

"Who's taking his part?" retorted Mr. Badger sharply. "I'm not going to uphold him in attacking Andrew, but I'm rather surprised at his mustering spunk enough to do it. As for his doing us any harm, that's all nonsense."

"You may change your mind when it's too late, Mr. Badger."

"Are you afraid of him?" asked her husband contemptuously as he regarded the tall, muscular figure of his wife, who probably would have been a match for himself in physical strength.

"I can defend myself if I am awake," said Mrs. Badger. "But what's to hinder his attacking me when I'm asleep?"

"You can fasten your door if you are afraid. But that isn't my trouble with him. There's something more serious, Mrs. B."

"What is it? What's he been doin'?"

"It isn't he. It's Charles Waldo. I'm free to say that Mr. Waldo is the meanest man I ever had dealings with. You know I wrote to him to see if he wouldn't allow me something extra toward the boy's keep."

"Yes."

"Well, read that letter. Or, stay, I'll read it to you."

Mr. Badger took the letter from his pocket and read it aloud to his wife and son. Mrs. Badger was as much disappointed as her husband, for she was quite as fond of money as he.

"What are you goin' to do?" she asked.

"I can't do anything," answered Mr. Badger in deep disgust.

"Will you keep the boy?"

"Of course I will. Between ourselves, he more than earns his victuals; but, all the same, Mr. Waldo is perfectly able to allow us a little profit."

"You must make him work harder," suggested Mrs. Badger.

"I mean to. Now, we will settle about this little affair. Where is Bill?"

"Out in the field, digging potatoes," said Andrew glibly.

"Go and call him."

"All right, sir."

And the boy prepared to obey the command with uncommon alacrity.

Poor Bill, nervous and unhappy, had been hard at work in the potato field through the long forenoon, meditating bitterly on his sad position. So far as he knew, there was no one that loved him, no one that cared for him. He was a friendless boy. From Mr. and Mrs. Badger and Andrew he never received a kind nor encouraging word, but, instead, taunts and reproaches, and the heart of the poor boy, hungering for kindness, found none.

"Will it always be so?" he asked himself. "If Andrew would only be kind to me I would do anything for him, but he seems to hate me, and so does Mrs. Badger. Mr. Badger isn't quite so bad, but he only cares for the work I do."

The poor boy sighed heavily as he leaned for a moment upon his hoe. "He was roused by a sharp voice.

"Shirking your work, are you?" said Andrew. "I've caught you this time. What'll my father say to that?"

"I have been working hard, Andrew," said Bill. "I can show you what I have done this forenoon."

"That's too thin. You're lazy, and that's all about it. Well, my father's got home, and now you're going to catch it. Maybe you'll knock him down with a hoe," said Andrew tauntingly.

"I'm sorry I hit you, Andrew, as I told you; but you shouldn't have struck me with a whip."

"I had a perfect right to do it. I'm your master."

"No, you're not!" returned Bill with spirit.

"We'll see whether I am or not. Come right up to the house."

"Who says so?"

"My father told me to call you."

"Very well, I will come," and the bound boy shouldered his hoe and followed Andrew wearily to the farmhouse yard, where Mr. and Mrs. Badger were standing.

One look at the stern faces of the pair satisfied Bill that trouble awaited him. He knew very well that he could not hope for justice and that one word from Andrew in the mind of his parents would outweigh all he could say.

"Here comes the young ruffian!" said Mrs. Badger as soon as he came within hearing distance. "Here comes the wicked boy who tried to kill my poor Andrew."

"That is not true, Mrs. Badger," said Bill earnestly. "I was only defending myself."

"You hear, Mr. Badger. He as much as tells me I lie! Do you hear that?" demanded the incensed woman.

"Bill Benton," said Mr. Badger sternly, "I hear you have made a savage and brutal attack on Andrew Jackson. Now, what have you to say for yourself, sir?"

"He struck me twice with a whip, Mr. Badger, and I got mad. I didn't mean to hurt him."

"You might have killed him!" broke in Mrs. Badger.

"No, I wouldn't, ma'am."

"Contradicting me again! If there was ever a boy looked like a young fiend, you did when I came out to save my boy from your brutal temper. Oh, you'll swing on the gallows some day, sir! I'm sure of that."

To an unprejudiced observer all this would have been very ridiculous. The delicate, refined-looking boy, whose face showed unmistakable gentleness and mildness, almost carried to an extreme, was about the last boy to whom such words could suitably have been addressed.

"Andrew Jackson, did you strike Bill with a whip?" asked Mr. Badger, turning to his son.

"No, I didn't," answered Andrew without a blush.

"How can you tell such a lie?" said Bill indignantly.

"Mr. Badger, will you allow this young ruffian to accuse your own son of falsehood?" cried the mother.

"Did you have a whip in your hand, Andrew?" asked his father.

Andrew hesitated a moment, but finally thought it best to say he did.

"Did you strike Bill with it?"

"No."

"You see how candid the poor boy is," said his mother. "He tells you that he had a whip in his hand, though many boys would have denied it. But my Andrew was always truthful."

Even Andrew felt a little embarrassed at this undeserved tribute to a virtue in which he knew that he was very deficient.

"Bill Benton," said Mr. Badger sternly, "it appears that you have not only made an atrocious assault on my son, but lied deliberately about it. You shall have neither dinner nor supper, and tonight I will give you a flogging. Now, go back to your work!"

"Ho, ho! You'll hit me again, will you?" said Andrew triumphantly as the poor boy slowly retraced his way to the field.

As the bound boy walked wearily back to the field he felt that he had little to live for. Hard work—too hard for his slender strength—accompanied by poor fare and cruel treatment, constituted his only prospect. But there seemed no alternative. He must keep on working and suffering—so far he could foresee.

He worked an hour and then he began to feel faint. He had eaten but little breakfast and he needed a fresh supply of food to restore his strength. How he could hold out till evening he could not tell. Already his head began to ache and he felt weary and listless.

He was left to work alone, for Mr. Badger usually indulged himself in the luxury of an after-dinner nap, lasting till at least three o'clock.

As he was plodding along suddenly he heard his name called in a cheery voice:

"Hello, Bill!"

Looking up, he saw Dick Schmidt, the son of a neighbor, a good-natured boy, whom he looked upon as almost his only friend.

"Hello, Dick!" he responded.

"You're looking pale, Bill," said his friend. "What's the matter?"

"I don't feel very well, Dick."

"You ought not to be at work. Have you had dinner?"

"I am not to have any."

"Why not?" asked Dick, opening his eyes. "I knew old Badger was mean, but I didn't think he was mean enough for that!"

"It's a punishment," Bill explained.

"What for?"

"For hitting Andrew Jackson with a hoe and knocking him down."

"Did you do that, Bill?" exclaimed Dick in great delight, for he disliked Mr. Badger's petted heir. "I didn't think it was in you! Shake hands, old fellow, and tell me all about it."

"I am afraid it was wicked, Dick, but I couldn't help it. I must have hurt him, for he screamed very loud."

"Better and better! I know how he treats you, Bill, and I tell you it'll do him good—the young tyrant! But you haven't told me about it."

Bill told the story, to which Dick listened with earnest attention. He expressed hearty approval of Bill's course and declared that he would have done the same.

"So you are in disgrace," he said. "Never mind. Bill. It'll all come out right. It is worth something to have punished that young bully. But what's the matter, Bill? What makes you so pale?"

"I think it's going without my dinner. The hard work makes me hungry."

"Just wait a minute. I'll be back in a jiffy!"

Dick was off like a shot. When he returned he brought with him two slices of bread and butter, a slice of cold meat and two apples.

"Eat 'em, Bill," he said. "They'll make you feel better."

"Oh, Dick! I didn't want to trouble you so much."

"It was no trouble, old fellow."

"What will your mother say to your taking all this?"

"She'll be glad of it. She isn't so mean as Mrs. Badger. I say, Bill, you must come over and take supper with us some time. There's plenty to eat at our house."

"I should like to, Dick, if Mr. Badger would let me."

"Don't talk any more till you have eaten what I brought you."

Bill obeyed his friend's directions, and, to Dick's great satisfaction, ate all that had been brought him with evident appetite.

"I feel a good deal better," he said as he took the hoe once more and set to work. "I feel strong now."

"It's lucky I came along. I say. Bill, is that your only punishment?"

A shadow came over Bill's face.

"I am to be flogged this evening," he said. "Mr. Badger told me so, and he always keeps his word."

Dick set his teeth and clinched his fists.

"I'd like to flog old Badger," he said energetically. "Are you going to stand it?"

"I can't help it, Dick."

"I'd help it!" said his friend, nodding emphatically.

Bill shook his head despondently.

The whipping seemed to him inevitable, and there seemed to be no way of avoiding it.

"What time do you expect he will whip you—the old brute?" asked Dick.

"He waits till nine o'clock, just after I have gone to bed."

"Then will you follow my advice?"

"What is it?"

Dick whispered in Bill's ear the plan he had in view. There was no need to whisper, but he did it to show that the communication was confidential.

This was the plan:

Bill was to go to bed as usual, but in about fifteen minutes he was to get out of the window, slide along the roof of the L and descend to the ground, when Dick was to meet him, escort him to his house and allow him to share his room for the night.

"Then," said he, "when the old man comes up to tackle you he'll have to pound the bed and get his satisfaction out of that. Won't that be a splendid joke?"

Bill smiled faintly. It seemed to him a daring defiance of Mr. Badger, but, after all, he wouldn't fare any worse than he was sure of doing, and he finally acquiesced, though with serious doubts as to the propriety of the plan.

"Don't say a word to let 'em know what you're going to do. Bill—mind that!"

"No, I won't."

"You'll be sure to find me waiting for you outside the house, just at the back of the barn. I'll give you some supper when you reach the house."

When the bound boy came from work in the evening he met stern, cold looks from Mr. and Mrs. Badger, but Andrew Jackson wore a look of triumphant malice. He was gloating over the punishment in reserve for the boy whom he so groundlessly hated.

"Ain't you hungry?" he said tauntingly.

Bill looked at him, but did not answer.

"Oh, you needn't answer. I know you are," said the young tyrant. "You didn't like it very much, going without your dinner. You ain't going to have any supper, either. If you're very hungry, though, and will go down on your knees and beg my pardon, I'll get you something to eat. What do you say?"

"I won't do what you say," said Bill slowly. "I don't care enough for supper to do that."

"You don't?" exclaimed Andrew angrily. "So you're stubborn, are you? Anyhow, you can't say I haven't given you a chance."

"You're very kind!" said the bound boy sarcastically, in spite of his gentleness.

"Of course I am," blustered Andrew Jackson. "Most boys wouldn't be, after the way you treated me."

"You want the satisfaction of having me beg your pardon," said Bill, looking full in the face of the petty despot.

"Yes, I do; and I mean to have it."

"You can, upon one condition."

"What's that?" asked Andrew Jackson, his curiosity overcoming his indignation.

"If you'll beg my pardon for striking me with your whip, I'll beg yours for hitting you with the hoe."

Andrew fairly gasped for breath at this daring proposal, and he looked for a moment as if he were in danger of having a stroke of apoplexy.

"You saucy beggar!" he ejaculated. "How dare you talk to me in that impertinent way? I'll tell father to give you the worst flogging ever you had to-night—see if I don't!"

And the boy left to report Bill's new insolence to his mother.

Bill crept up to bed a little earlier than usual. He knew that Mr. Badger would not ascend to his humble room to administer the threatened punishment till nine o'clock or later.

Through a refinement of cruelty that humane gentleman chose to let his intended victim lie in an anxious anticipation of the flogging, thus making it assume greater terror.

In fact, he probably would not return from the village till nine o'clock or later, and this was an additional reason why he put it off.

His absence made it easier for Bill to carry out the plan which had been formed for him by his trusty friend, Dick Schmidt, and escape from the house.

He accomplished his escape unnoticed about half-past eight o'clock.

Dick was waiting for him behind the barn. He had been a little afraid that Bill would repent the promise he had made and back out. When he saw him he welcomed him gladly.

"I was afraid you wouldn't dare to come, Bill," he said.

"I shan't be any worse off," said the bound boy. "Mr. Badger was going to give me a flogging, anyway, and he can't do any more than that as it is."

"What an old brute he is!" exclaimed Dick.

"He isn't as bad as his wife or Andrew Jackson."

"That's so! Andrew is a mean boy. I'm glad you hit him."

"I am sorry, Dick."

"Don't you think he deserved it?"

"Yes, but I don't like to be the one to do it."

"I wouldn't mind it," said Dick, "but he's precious careful not to get into any muss with me."

"You're not bound to Mr. Badger."

"If I were, he wouldn't dare to order me round. Catch him bulldozing me!"

"You're more plucky than I am, Dick."

"You're too good-natured, Bill—that's what's the matter with you."

"I hate fighting, Dick."

"What did Andrew say to you when you came home from work?"

"He wanted me to go down on my knees and beg his pardon for hitting him."

"Why didn't you knock him down?" said Dick quickly.

"I told him I'd do it——"

"What!" exclaimed Dick Schmidt in the deepest disgust.

"If he'd beg my pardon first for striking me with a whip."

"That's better. I thought you wouldn't be so much of a coward as to beg his pardon."

"He didn't accept the offer," said Bill, smiling.

"No, I suppose not. Was he mad?"

"He looked as if he was. He called me a saucy beggar and threatened to tell his father."

"I've no doubt he will. He's just mean enough to do that. I say, Bill, it's a pity you don't work for my father."

"I wish I did, Dick, but perhaps you'd boss me, too."

64

"Not much danger. We'd be like brothers."

While this conversation was going on the two boys were walking across the fields to Mr. Schmidt's farm. The distance was not great, and by this time they were at the back door.

As they went in Bill's eyes glistened as he saw a nice supper laid on the kitchen table, waiting for him, for Dick had told his mother of the guest he expected. He decided to say nothing of the circumstances that led to the invitation. He might safely have done so, however, for Mrs. Schmidt was a good, motherly woman, who pitied the boy and understood very well that his position in Mr. Badger's family must be a very disagreeable one.

"I am glad to see you, William," she said. "Sit right down and eat supper. I've got a hot cup of tea for you."

"I'll sit down, too, mother. I only ate a little supper, for I wanted to keep Bill company."

Presently the boys went to bed and had a social chat before going to sleep.

"I wish," said Dick, "I could be where I could look on when old Badger goes up to your room and finds the bird flown."

If Dick could have been there, he would have witnessed an extraordinary scene.

CHAPTER XXIX

THE BATTLE IN THE ATTIC

About ten minutes after Bill Benton left his little chamber an ill-looking man, whose garb and general appearance made it clear that he was a tramp, came strolling across the fields. He had made some inquiries about the farmers in the neighborhood, and his attention was drawn to Nathan Badger as a man who was likely to keep money in the house.

Some tramps are honest men, the victims of misfortune, not of vice, but Tom Tapley belonged to a less creditable class. He had served two terms in a State penitentiary without deriving any particular moral benefit from his retired life therein. His ideas on the subject of honesty were decidedly loose, and none who knew him well would have trusted him with the value of a dollar.

Such was the man who approached the Badger homestead.

Now it happened that Mrs. Badger and Andrew Jackson had gone to make a call. Both intended to be back by nine o'clock, as neither wished to lose the gratification of being near by when Bill Benton received his flogging. As for Mr. Badger, he was at the village as usual in the evening.

Thus it will be seen that as Bill also had left the house, no one was left in charge.

Tom Tapley made a careful examination of the house from the outside, and his experienced eyes discovered that it was unprotected.

"Here's luck!" he said to himself. "Now what's to prevent my explorin' this here shanty and makin' off with any valuables I come across?"

Two objections, however, occurred to the enterprising tramp: First, it was not likely at that time in the evening that he would be left alone long enough to gather in his booty, and, secondly, the absent occupants of the house might have money and articles of value on their persons which at present it would be impossible to secure.

The front door was not locked. Mr. Tapley opened it, and, finding the coast clear, went upstairs. Continuing his explorations, he made his way to the little attic chamber usually occupied by the bound boy.

"Nobody sleeps here, I expect, though the bed is rumpled," he said to himself. "There's two boys, I've heard, but it's likely they sleep together downstairs. I guess I'll slip into bed and get a little rest till it's time to attend to business."

The tramp, with a sigh of enjoyment, for he had not lately slept in a bed, lay down on Bill's hard couch. It was not long before drowsiness overcame him and he fell asleep.

In the meantime the three absent members of the family came home. First Mrs. Badger and Andrew Jackson returned from their visit.

"Your father isn't home yet, Andrew," said his mother.

"I hope he will come soon, for I'm sleepy," said Andrew.

"Then you had better go to bed, my darling."

"No, I won't. I ain't goin' to lose seein' Bill's flogging. I hope father'll lay it on well."

"No doubt the boy deserves it."

"What do you think he had the impudence to say to me, mother?" asked Andrew.

"I shall not be surprised at any impudence from the young reprobate."

"He wanted me to beg his pardon for strikin' him with a whip, as he said I did."

"Well, I never did!" ejaculated Mrs. Badger. "To think of my boy apologizing to a low, hired boy like him!"

65

"Oh, he's gettin' awful airy, ma! Shouldn't wonder if he thought he was my equal!"

"There's nothing but a flogging will subdue such a boy as that. I ain't unmerciful, and if the boy showed a proper humility I wouldn't mind doin' all I could for him and overlookin' his faults, but when he insults my Andrew, I can't excuse him. But there's one thing I can't understand: He didn't use to be so bold."

"I know what has changed him, ma."

"What is it, Andrew?"

"It's that Dick Schmidt. Dick treats him as if he was his equal, and that makes him put on airs."

"Then Dick lowers himself—though, to be sure, I don't hold him to be equal to you! The Badgers are a better family than the Schmidts, and so are the Coneys, which was my name before I was married."

"I wonder whether Bill's asleep?" said Andrew.

"You might go to the foot of the stairs and listen," said his mother.

Andrew followed his mother's advice, and, opening the door at the foot of the attic stairs, was astonished to hear the deep breathing which issued from Bill's chamber.

"Ma," he said, "Bill is snoring like a house afire."

"Reckless boy! Does he make so light of the flogging which your father has promised him?"

"I don't know. He's gettin' awful sassy lately. I do wish father would come home."

"I think I hear him now," said Mrs. Badger, listening intently.

Her ears did not deceive her.

Soon the steps of the master of the house, as he considered himself, were heard upon the doorstep, and Mr. Nathan Badger entered.

"I'm glad you've come, pa. Are you goin' to flog Bill now?"

"Yes, my son. Get me a stout stick from the woodshed."

Andrew Jackson obeyed with alacrity.

Armed with the stick, Mr. Badger crept upstairs, rather astonished by his bound boy's noisy breathing, and, entering the darkened chamber, brought the stick down smartly on the astonished sleeper.

In about two minutes Mrs. Badger and Andrew, standing at the foot of the stairs, were astonished by the noise of a terrible conflict in the little attic chamber, as if two men were wrestling.

There was the sound of a heavy body flung on the floor, and the voice of Mr. Badger was heard shouting:

"Help! help! murder!"

"The young villain's killing your father!" exclaimed the astonished Mrs. Badger. "Go up and help him!"

"I don't dare to," said Andrew, pale as a sheet.

"Then I will!" said his mother, and she hurried upstairs, only to be met by her husband, who was literally tumbled downstairs by the occupant of the attic chamber.

Husband and wife fell together in a heap, and Andrew Jackson uttered a yell of dismay.

In all the confidence of assured victory, Mr. Nathan Badger, seeing the dim outline of a figure upon the bed, had brought down his stick upon it with emphasis.

"I'll l'arn you!" he muttered in audible accents.

It was a rude awakening for Tom Tapley, the tramp, who was sleeping as peacefully as a child.

The first blow aroused him, but left him in a state of bewilderment, so that he merely shrank from the descending stick without any particular idea of what had happened to him.

"Didn't feel it, did yer?" exclaimed Mr. Badger. "Well, I'll see if I can't make yer feel it!" and he brought down the stick for the second time with considerably increased vigor.

By this time Tom Tapley was awake. By this time also he thoroughly understood the situation or thought he did. He had been found out, and the farmer had undertaken to give him a lesson.

"That depends on whether you're stronger than I am," thought Tom, and he sprang from the bed and threw himself upon the astonished farmer.

Nathan Badger was almost paralyzed by the thought that Bill Benton, his hired boy, was absolutely daring enough to resist his lawful master. He was even more astounded by Bill's extraordinary strength. Why, as the boy grappled with him, he actually felt powerless. He was crushed to the floor, and, with the boy's knee upon his breast, struggled in vain to get up. It was so dark that he had not yet discovered that his antagonist was a man and not a boy.

66

Nathan Badger had heard that insane persons are endowed with extraordinary strength, and it flashed upon him that the boy had become suddenly insane.

The horror of being in conflict with a crazy boy so impressed him that he cried for help.

Then it was that Tom Tapley, gathering all his strength, lifted up the prostrate farmer and pitched him downstairs just as Mrs. Badger was mounting them, so that she and her husband fell in a breathless heap on the lower stairs, to the indescribable dismay of Andrew Jackson.

Mrs. Badger was the first to pick herself up.

"What does all this mean, Mr. Badger?" she asked.

"That's what I'd like to know," said Mr. Badger ruefully.

"You don't mean to say you ain't a match for a boy?" she demanded sarcastically.

"Perhaps you'd like to try him yourself?" said her husband.

"This is very absurd, Mr. Badger. You know very well he's weak for a boy of sixteen, and he hasn't had anything to eat since morning."

"If you think he's weak, you'd better tackle him," retorted Nathan. "I tell you, wife, he's got the strength of a man and a strong man, too."

"I don't understand it. Tell me exactly what happened."

"Well, you saw me go upstairs with the stick Andrew Jackson gave me," said Mr. Badger, assuming a sitting position. "I saw the boy lyin' on the bed, snoring and I up with my stick and brought it down pretty hard. He quivered a little, but that was all. So I thought I'd try it again. He jumped out of bed and sprang on me like a tiger, grinding his teeth, but not saying a word. I tell you, wife, he seemed as strong as a horse. I couldn't get up, and he sat and pounded me."

"The idea of being pounded by a small boy!" ejaculated Mrs. Badger.

"Just what I'd have said a quarter of an hour ago!"

"It seems impossible!"

"Perhaps it does, but it's so."

"He never acted so before."

"No, and he never hit Andrew Jackson before, but yesterday he did it. I tell you what, wife, I believe the boy's gone crazy."

"Crazy!" ejaculated Mrs. Badger and Andrew in a breath.

"Just so! When folks are crazy they're a good deal stronger than it's nateral for them to be, and that's the way with Bill Benton."

"But what could possibly make him crazy?" demanded Mrs. Badger incredulously.

"It may be the want of vittles. I don't know as we'd orter have kept him without his dinner and supper."

"I don't believe a bit in such rubbish," said Mrs. Badger, whose courage had come back with the absolute silence in the attic chamber. "I believe you're a coward, Nathan Badger. I'll go upstairs myself and see if I can't succeed better than you did."

"You'd better not, wife."

"Oh, don't go, ma!" said Andrew Jackson, pale with terror.

"I'm going!" said the intrepid woman. "It shan't be said of me that I'm afraid of a little bound boy who's as weak as a rat."

"You'll find out how weak he is," said Mr. Badger. "I warn you not to go."

"I'm goin', all the same," said Mrs. Badger. "You'll see how I'll tame him down. Give me the stick."

"Then go if you're so plaguy obstinate," said her husband, and it must be confessed that he rather hoped his wife, who had ventured to ridicule him, might herself meet with a reception that would make her change her tune somewhat.

Mrs. Badger, stick in hand, marched up to the door of the attic and called out boldly:

"Open the door, you young villain!"

"How does she know I'm young?" thought Tom Tapley, who was on guard in the room. "Well, now, if she wasn't such an old woman I should feel flattered. I guess I'll have to scare her a little. It wouldn't be polite to tumble her downstairs as I did her husband."

"Have you gone crazy?" demanded Mrs. Badger behind the door.

"Not that I know of," muttered the tramp.

"Perhaps you think you can manage me as well as Mr. Badger?" she continued.

"I should smile if I couldn't," commented Tom Tapley. "That woman must think she's extra strong to be a match for me!"

"I'm coming in to whip you till you cry for mercy!"

"Really, she's a pretty spunky old woman!" thought the tramp. "If I can't hold my own against her, I'll sell myself for old rags!"

Mrs. Badger pushed open the door, saw dimly the outline of the tramp and struck at it with the stick.

But alas! the stick was wrenched from her hand, a pistol, loaded only with powder, was discharged, and the intrepid lady, in a panic, flew out of the room and downstairs, tumbling into her husband's arms.

Nathan Badger was delighted at his wife's discomfiture. She couldn't taunt him any longer.

"I told you so!" he chuckled. "How do you like tacklin' him yourself, my dear? Wouldn't you like to try it again? Ho! ho!"

"Mr. Badger, you're a fool!" exclaimed his wife sharply.

"It strikes me you're a little in that way yourself, Mrs. Badger. Did you give him a floggin'? Ho, ho! you were in a great hurry to come away!"

"Mr. Badger, he fired at me with a pistol. I tell you he's a dangerous boy to have in the house."

"Oh, no, Mrs. Badger, you can manage him just as easy!"

"Shut up, Mr. Badger! How did I know he had a pistol? I tell you it's a serious thing! Before morning, you, and Andrew Jackson, and me may be dead corpses!"

At this awful statement Andrew Jackson burst into a terrified howl.

"I'll tell you what we'd better do, Mr. Badger. We'll go into our room and lock ourselves in."

"Let me come in, too," said Andrew. "He'll kill me! He hates me!"

"Yes, my darling, you may come, too!" said his mother.

So the valiant three locked themselves up in a chamber and listened nervously.

But Tom Tapley was already out of the house. He made his escape over the roof, fearing that the neighborhood would be roused and his safety endangered.

So passed a night of unparalleled excitement in the Badger homestead.

CHAPTER XXX

ATTACKED IN THE REAR

Early the next morning the three Badgers held a council of war.

It was unanimously decided that something must be done, but what that something should be it was not easy to determine.

Mr. Badger suggested that the town constable should be summoned.

"The boy has committed assault and battery upon our persons, Mrs. Badger," he said, "and it is proper that he should be arrested."

"Shall I go for the constable?" asked Andrew Jackson. "I should like to have him put in jail. Then we should be safe."

"The constable would not be up so early, Andrew."

"Besides," said Mrs. Badger, "we shall be laughed at for not being able to take care of a single small-sized boy."

"You know what he is capable of, Mrs. Badger. At least you did when you came flyin' down the attic stairs into my arms!"

"Shut up, Mr. Badger," said his wife, who was ashamed when she remembered her panic. "You'd better not say anything. He got you on the floor and pounded you—you a full-grown man!"

"I'd like to pound him!" said Badger, setting his teeth hard.

"It's a pity if three of us can't manage him without calling in a constable," continued Mrs. Badger, who, on the whole, had more courage than her husband.

"What do you propose, wife?" asked Nathan.

"I propose that we all go up and seize him. He is probably asleep and can't give any trouble. We can tie him hand and foot before he wakes up."

"Capital!" said Mr. Badger, who was wonderfully assured by the thought that his young enemy might be asleep. "We'll go right up."

"He may be awake!" suggested Andrew Jackson.

"True. We must go well armed. I'll carry the gun. It will do to knock the pistol out of his hand before he gets a chance to use it."

"Perhaps so," assented Mrs. Badger.

"And you, Andrew Jackson, what can you take?"

"I'll take the poker," said the heroic Andrew.

"Very good! We had better arm ourselves as soon as possible or he may wake up. By the way, Mr. Badger, where is the ball of twine? It will be useful to tie the boy's hands."

"If his hands are tied he can't work."

"No, but I will only keep them tied while I give him a thrashing. You can take possession of his pistol and hide it. When he is thoroughly subdued we will untie him and send him to work."

"Without his breakfast?" suggested Andrew.

"No, he has already fasted since yesterday morning, and it may make him desperate. He shall have some breakfast, and that will give him strength to work."

Andrew Jackson was rather disappointed at the decision that Bill was to have breakfast, but on this point he did not venture to oppose his father.

The plan of campaign having been decided upon, it only remained to carry it out.

Mr. Badger took the old musket and headed the procession. His wife slipped downstairs and returned with the kitchen broom and a poker. The last she put in the hands of her son.

"Use it, Andrew Jackson, if occasion requires. You may be called upon to defend your father and mother. Should such be the case, do not flinch, but behave like a hero."

"I will, ma!" exclaimed Andrew, fired perhaps by the example of the great general after whom he was named. "But you and pa must tackle him first."

"We will!" exclaimed the intrepid matron. "The disgraceful scenes of last evening must not again be enacted. This time we march to certain victory. Mr. Badger, go on, and I will follow."

The three, in the order arranged, advanced to the foot of the stairs, and Mr. Badger slowly and cautiously mounted them, pausing before the door of the room that contained, as he supposed, the desperate boy.

"Shall I speak to him before entering?" he asked in a tone of indecision, turning back to his wife.

"Certainly not; it will put him on his guard. Keep as still as you can.
We want to surprise him."

To account for what followed it must be stated that Dick Schmidt awakened his visitor early and the two went down to breakfast. Mr. Schmidt was going to the market town and found it necessary to breakfast at five o'clock. This happened fortunately for Bill, as he was able to obtain a much better breakfast there than at home.

When breakfast was over he said soberly:
"Dick, I must go back."
"Why do you go back at all?" said Dick impulsively.
"I must. It is the only home I have."
"I wish you could stay with me."
"So do I, but Mr. Badger would come after me."
"I suppose he would. Do you think he will flog you?"
"I am sure he will."
"I'd like to flog him—the brute! Don't take it too hard, Bill. You'll be a man some time, and then no one can punish you."

Poor Bill! As he took his lonely way back to the house of his tyrannical employer in the early morning he could not help wishing that he was already a man and his days of thraldom were over. He was barely sixteen. Five long, weary years lay before him.

"I'll try to stand it, though it's hard," murmured Bill. "I suppose he's very mad because I wasn't home last night. But I'm glad I went. I had two good meals and a quiet night's sleep."

It was not long before he came in sight of home.

Probably no one was up in the Badger household. Usually Bill was the first to get up and Mrs. Badger next, for Andrew Jackson and his father were neither of them fond of early rising.

The front and back doors were no doubt locked, but Bill knew how to get in.

He went to the shed, raised a window and clambered in.

"Perhaps I can get up to my room without anybody hearing me," he reflected.

He passed softly through the front room into the entry and up the front stairs. All was quiet. Bill concluded that no one was up. He came to the foot of the attic stairs, and his astonished gaze rested on the three Badgers, armed respectively with a gun, a broom and a poker, all on their way to his room.

"Were they going to murder me?" he thought.

Just then Andrew Jackson, who led the rear, and was therefore nearest to
Bill, looked back and saw the terrible foe within three feet of him.

He uttered a loud yell, and, scarcely knowing what he was about, brought down the poker with force on his mother's back, at the same time crying:

"There he is, ma!"

Mrs. Badger, in her flurry, struck her husband with the broom, while her husband, equally panic-stricken, fired the musket. It was overloaded, and, as a natural result, "kicked," overthrowing Mr. Badger, who in his downward progress carried with him his wife and son.

Astonished and terrified, Bill turned and fled, leaving the house in the same way he entered it. He struck across the fields and in that moment decided that he would never return to Mr. Badger unless he was dragged there. He felt sure that if he did he would be murdered.

He had no plans except to get away. He saw Dick Schmidt, bade him a hurried good-by and took the road toward the next town.

For three days he traveled, indebted to compassionate farmers for food. But excitement and fatigue finally overcame him, and he sank by the roadside, about fifty miles from the town of Dexter, whence he had started on his pilgrimage.

CHAPTER XXXI
BILL BENTON FINDS A FRIEND

Late one afternoon Robert Coverdale reached Columbus on his Western trip. The next day he was to push on to the town of Dexter, where he had information that the boy of whom he was in search lived.

The train, however, did not leave till eleven o'clock in the forenoon, and Robert felt justified in devoting his leisure hours to seeing what he could of the city and its surroundings.

He took an early breakfast and walked out into the suburbs.

As he strolled along a little boy, about seven years old, ran to meet him.

"Please, mister," he said, "won't you come quick? There's a boy layin' by the road back there, and I guess he's dead!"

Robert needed no second appeal. His heart was warm and he liked to help others when he could.

"Show me where, bub," he said.

The little fellow turned and ran back, Robert keeping pace with him.

By the roadside, stretched out, pale and with closed eyes, lay the poor bound boy, known as Bill Benton.

He was never very strong, and the scanty fare to which he had been confined had sapped his physical strength.

Robert, at first sight, thought he was dead. He bent down and put his hand upon the boy's heart. It was beating, though faintly.

"Is he dead, mister?" asked the boy.

"No, but he has fainted away. Is there any water near by?"

Yes, there was a spring close at hand, the little boy said.

Robert ran to it, soaked his handkerchief in it, and, returning, laved the boy's face. The result was encouraging.

Bill opened his eyes and asked in a wondering tone:

"Where am I?"

"You are with a friend," said Robert soothingly. "How do you feel?"

"I am very tired and weak," murmured Bill.

"Are you traveling?"

"Yes."

"Where?"

"I don't know."

Robert thought that the boy's mind might be wandering, but continued:

"Have you no friends in Columbus?"

"No. I have no friends anywhere!" answered Bill sorrowfully, "except Dick Schmidt."

"I suppose Dick is a boy?"

"Yes."

"Where have you been living?"

"You won't take me back there?" said Bill uneasily.

"I won't take you anywhere where you don't want to go. I want to be your friend, if you will let me."

"I should like a friend," answered Bill slowly. Then, examining the kind, boyish face that was bent over him, he said, "I like you."

"Have you had anything to eat to-day?" asked Robert.

"No."

"Will you go with me to my hotel?"

"I have no money."

"Poor boy!" thought Robert, "it is easy enough to see that."

Bill's ragged clothes were assurance enough of the truth of what he said.

"I must take care of this poor boy," thought Robert. "It will delay me, but I can't leave him."

He heard the sound of approaching wheels, and, looking up, saw a man approaching in a wagon. Robert signaled him to stop.

70

"I want to take this boy to the hotel," he said, "but he has not strength enough to walk. Will you take us aboard? I will pay you a fair price."

"Poor little chap! He looks sick, that's a fact!" said the kind-hearted countryman. "Yes, I'll give you both a lift, and I won't ask a cent."

There was some surprise felt at the hotel when Robert appeared with his new-found friend. Some of the servants looked askance at the ragged clothes, but Robert said quietly:

"I will pay for him," and no objection was made.

When Bill was undressed and put to bed and had partaken of a refreshing breakfast he looked a great deal brighter and seemed much more cheerful.

"You are very kind," he said to Robert.

"I hope somebody would do as much for me if I needed it," answered Robert. "Do you mind telling me about yourself?"

"I will tell anything you wish," said Bill, who now felt perfect confidence in his new friend.

"What is your name?"

"Bill Benton; at any rate, that's what they call me."

"Don't you think it's your real name, then?"

"No."

"Have you any remembrance of your real name?" asked Robert, not dreaming of the answer he would receive.

"When I was a little boy they called me Julian, but——"

"Julian!" repeated Robert eagerly.

"Yes."

"Can you tell what was your last name?" asked Robert quickly.

Bill shook his head.

"No, I don't remember."

"Tell me," said Robert, "did you live with a man named Badger in the town of Dexter?"

The sick boy started and seemed extremely surprised.

"How did you find out?" he asked. "Did Mr. Badger send you for me?"

"I never saw Mr. Badger in my life."

Bill—er perhaps I ought to say Julian—looked less anxious.

"Yes," he said, "but he treated me badly and I ran away."

"Did you ever hear of a man named Charles Waldo?"

"Yes, he was the man that sent me to Mr. Badger."

"It's a clear case!" thought Robert, overjoyed, "I have no doubt now that I have found the hermit's son. Poor boy, how he must have suffered!"

"Julian," said he, "do you know why I am traveling—what brought me here? But of course you don't. I came to find you."

"To find me? But you said——"

"No, it was not Mr. Badger nor Mr. Waldo that sent me. They are your enemies. The one that sent me is your friend. Julian, how would you like to have a father?"

"My father is dead."

"Who told you so?"

"Mr. Waldo. He told Mr. Badger so."

"He told a falsehood, then. You have a father, and as soon as you are well enough I'll take you to him."

"Will he be kind to me?"

"Do not fear. For years he has grieved for you, supposing you dead. Once restored to him, you will have everything to make you happy. Your father is a rich man, and you won't be overworked again."

"What is my father's name?" asked Julian.

"His name is Gilbert Huet."

"Huet! Yes, that's the name!" exclaimed Julian eagerly. "I remember it now. My name used to be Julian Huet, but Mr. Waldo was always angry whenever any one called me by that name, and so he changed it to Bill Benton."

"He must be a great scoundrel," said Robert. "Now, Julian, I will tell you my plan. I don't believe there is anything the matter with you except the want of rest and good food. You shall have both. You also want some new clothes."

"Yes," said Julian, looking at the ragged suit which now hung over a chair. "I should like some new clothes."

A doctor was called, who confirmed Robert's opinion.

"The youngster will be all right in a week or ten days," he said. "All he wants is rest and good living."

"How soon will he be able to travel?"

"In a week, at the outside."

During this week Robert's attention was drawn to the following paragraph in a copy of the Dexter Times, a small weekly paper, which he found in the reading room of the hotel:

"A DESPERATE YOUNG RUFFIAN.—We understand that a young boy in the service of Mr. Nathan Badger, one of our most respected citizens, has disappeared under very extraordinary circumstances. The evening previous to his departure he made an unprovoked attack upon Mr. and Mrs. Badger, actually throwing Mr. Badger downstairs and firing a pistol at Mrs. Badger. He was a small, slight boy, but the strength he exhibited was remarkable in thus coping successfully with a strong man. Mr. Badger thinks the boy must have been suddenly attacked by insanity of a violent character."

"What does this mean, Julian?" asked Robert, reading the paragraph to his young protege.

"I don't know," answered Julian, astonished. "I spent the last night before I came away with my friend Dick Schmidt."

In a few days Julian looked quite another boy. His color began to return and his thin form to fill out, while his face wore a peaceful and happy expression.

In a new and handsome suit of clothes he looked like a young gentleman and not at all like Bill Benton, the bound boy. He was devotedly attached to Robert, the more so because he had never before—as far as his memory went—received so much kindness from any one as from him.

"Now," thought Robert, "I am ready to go back to Cook's Harbor and restore Julian to his father."

CHAPTER XXXII
ONCE MORE IN COOK'S HARBOR

Various had been the conjectures in Cook's Harbor as to what had become of Robert Coverdale.

Upon this point the hermit was the only person who could have given authentic information, but no one thought of applying to him.

Naturally questions were put to Mrs. Trafton, but she herself had a very vague idea of Robert's destination, and, moreover, she had been warned not to be communicative.

Mr. Jones, the landlord, supposed he had gone to try to raise the amount of his mortgage among distant relatives, but on this point he felt no anxiety.

"He won't succeed," said he to his wife; "you may depend on that. I don't believe he's got any relations that have money, and, even if he has, they're goin' to think twice before they give a boy two hundred dollars on the security of property they don't know anything about."

"What do you intend to do with the cottage, Mr. Jones?"

"It's worth five hundred dollars, and I can get more than the interest of five hundred dollars in the way of rent."

"Is anybody likely to hire it?"

"John Shelton's oldest son talks of getting married. He'll be glad to hire it of me."

"What's to become of Mrs. Trafton?"

"I don't know and I don't care," answered the landlord carelessly. "The last time I called she was impudent to me; came near ordering me out of the house till I made her understand that I had more right to the house than she had."

"She puts on a good many airs for a poor woman," said Mrs. Jones. "It's too ridiculous for a woman like her to be proud."

"If anything, she isn't as bad as that young whelp. Bob Coverdale. The boy actually told me I wasn't respectful enough to his precious aunt. I wonder if they'll be respectful to her in the poorhouse—where it's likely she'll fetch up?"

"I don't see where the boy got money enough to go off," said Mrs. Jones.

"He didn't need much to get to Boston or New York. He's probably blackin' boots or sellin' papers in one of the two."

"I hope he is. I wonder how that sort of work will suit the young gentleman?"

"To-morrow the time's up, and I shall foreclose the mortgage. I'll fix up the place a little and then offer it to young Shelton. I guess he'll be willin' to pay me fifty dollars a year rent, and that'll be pretty good interest on my two hundred dollars."

"Have you given Mrs. Trafton any warning?"

"No, why should I? She knows perfectly well when the time is out, and she's had time to get the money. If she's got it, well and good, but if she hasn't, she can't complain. Oh, there's young Shelton," said the landlord, looking out of the window.

"I'll call him and see if we can make a bargain about renting the cottage."

"Frank Shelton!" called out Mr. Jones, raising the window.

The young fisherman paused.

"Come in; I want to speak to you."

Frank Shelton turned in from the street and the landlord commenced his attack.

"Frank, folks say you're thinkin' of gettin' married?"

"Maybe I shall," said the young man bashfully.

"Whereabouts do you cal'late to live?"

"Well, I don't know any place."

"What do you say to the Widder Trafton's house?"

"Is she goin' to leave?"

"I think she'll have to. Fact is, Frank, I've got a mortgage on the place which she can't pay, and I'll have to foreclose. You can have it as soon as you want it."

"How much rent did you cal'late to ask, Mr. Jones?"

"I'd ought to have five dollars a month, but, seein' it's you," said the politic landlord, "you may have it for fifty dollars a year."

"I'll speak to Nancy about it," said the young fisherman. "I don't want to turn Mrs. Trafton out, but if she's got to go, I suppose I might as well hire the house as any one else."

"Just so. I tell you, Frank, I'm offerin' you a bargain."

Just then Frank Shelton, who was looking out of the window, exclaimed in surprise:

"Why, there's Bob Coverdale!"

"Where?"

"He just walked by, with a smaller boy alongside."

"You don't say so!" uttered Mr. Jones, hardly knowing whether to be glad or sorry. "Well, he's come in time to bid good-by to his old home. I'll go up to-morrow, first thing, and settle this matter. I s'pose they'll try to beg off, but it won't be any use."

Robert had written to the hermit from Columbus a letter which conveyed the glad tidings of his success. It filled the heart of the recluse with a great and abounding joy.

Life seemed wholly changed for him. Now he felt that he had something to live for, and he determined to change his course of life entirely. He would move to Boston or New York and resume the social position which he had abandoned. There he would devote himself to the training and education of his boy.

And Robert—yes, he would richly reward the boy who had restored to him the son lost so long. He would not yet decide what he would do for him, but he felt that there was no reward too great for such a service.

He knew on what day to expect the two boys, for Robert had informed him by letter. Restless, he waited for the moment which should restore his son to his arms. He took a position on the beach in front of the entrance to the cave and looked anxiously for the approach of the two boys.

No longer was he clad in his hermit dress, but from a trunk he had drawn out a long-disused suit, made for him in other days by a fashionable tailor on Broadway, and he had carefully trimmed and combed his neglected locks.

"My boy must not be ashamed of my appearance," he said proudly. "My hermit life is over. Henceforth I will live as a man among men."

Presently his waiting glance was rewarded. Two boys, one of whom he recognized as Robert, descended the cliff and walked briskly toward him on the firm sand beach.

He did not wait now, but hurried toward them. He fixed his eyes eagerly upon the second boy.

Julian had much improved in appearance since we first made his acquaintance. It does not take long to restore strength and bloom into a boy of sixteen. He was slender still, but the hue of health mantled his cheeks; he was no longer sad, but hopeful, and in his delicate and refined features his father could see a strong resemblance to the wife he had lost.

"Julian!" said Robert Coverdale, "that's your father who is coming. Let him see that you are glad to meet him.

"Mr. Huet," he said, "this is your son."

"You do not need to tell me. He is too like his mother. Julian, my boy,
Heaven be praised that has restored you to me!"

It is hardly to be expected that Julian should feel the rapture that swelled the father's heart, for the thought of having a father at all was still new and strange, but it was not long before he learned to love him.

The poor boy had received so little kindness that his father's warm affection touched his heart, and he felt glad and happy to have such a protector.

"God bless and reward you, Robert!" said Mr. Huet, taking the hand of our hero. "You shall find that I am not ungrateful for this great service. I want to talk to my boy alone for a time, but I will come to your aunt's house to supper with Julian. Please tell her so, and ask her to let it be a good one."

"I will, Mr. Huet."

From Julian his father drew the story of his years of hardship and ill treatment, and his heart was stirred with indignation as he thought of the cruelty of the relative who had subjected him and his son to that long period of grief and suffering.

"Your trials are over now, Julian," he said. "You will be content to live with me, will you not?"

"Will Robert live with us?" asked the boy.

"Do you like Robert?" asked his father.

"I love him like a brother," said Julian impulsively. "You don't know how kind he has been to me, father!"

"Yes, Robert shall live with us, if he will," said Mr. Huet. "I will speak about it to him tomorrow."

"Will you live here, father?"

"Oh, no! You must be educated. I shall take you to Boston or New York, and there you shall have every advantage that money can procure. Hitherto I have not cared to be rich. Now, Julian, I value money for your sake."

Together they went to Mrs. Trafton's cottage to supper.

"What makes you look so sober, Robert?" asked Mr. Huet, observing that the boy looked grave.

"I have heard that Mr. Jones will foreclose his mortgage to-morrow."

"Not if you pay it," said Mr. Huet quietly. "Come with me after supper, and I will hand you all the money you require."

Robert was about to express his gratitude, but Mr. Huet stopped him.

"You owe me no thanks," he said. "It is only the first installment of a great debt which I can never wholly repay."

CHAPTER XXXIII

THE LANDLORD'S DEFEAT

About ten o'clock the next morning Mr. Nahum Jones approached the Trafton cottage.

Sitting on a bench outside was Robert Coverdale, whittling. He had put on his old clothes, intending it to be for the last time. He wanted to surprise Mr. Jones.

"There's Bob Coverdale," said Mr. Jones to himself. "He don't look much as if he was able to pay the mortgage. I guess I've got the place fast enough."

"Is your aunt at home, young man?" he said pompously.

"Yes," answered Robert, continuing to whittle.

"You might say 'yes, sir.'"

"All right. I'll remember next time."

"You'd better. Tell your aunt I want to see her—on business," emphasizing the last two words.

"Come right in, sir."

Mr. Jones, with a patronizing air, entered the house of which he already considered himself the proprietor.

Mrs. Trafton was engaged in making a pudding, for she had two boarders now, Julian and his father, who were to take their meals in the fisherman's cottage till they got ready to leave Cook's Harbor.

"Good mornin', ma'am," said Mr. Jones.

"Good morning. Will you take a seat?" she said quietly.

"I can't stay long, Mrs. Trafton. I called on a little matter of business."

"Very well, sir."

"I suppose you understand what it is?"

"Perhaps I do, but you had better explain."

"I have made up my mind to foreclose the mortgage I hold on this place, and I should like to have you move out within three days, as I am going to let it."

"Indeed! To whom do you intend to let it?"

"To Frank Shelton. He's goin' to be married, and this house will suit him."

"And what am I to do, Mr. Jones? You surely do not mean to deprive Robert and me of our home?"

"It isn't yours any longer, or won't be. Of course, you can't expect to stay here. I haven't forgotten how you talked to me when I was here before nor how impudent your boy was."

"Meaning me?" asked Robert with a grave face.

"Of course I mean you!" said Mr. Jones sharply.

"I haven't said anything impudent to you to-day, have I?"

"No, but you'd ought to have thought of that before. It's too late now!"

"You won't turn us out on the street, will you, Mr. Jones?"

"Haven't I given you three days to stay? If you want my advice, I should say that you'd find a good, comfortable home in the poorhouse. Your boy there might be bound out to a farmer."

"I don't know any farmer that wants a boy," said Robert meekly.

"I'd take you myself," said Nahum Jones, "if you wasn't so impudent. I'm afraid you're a little too airy for me."

"Wouldn't you let the house to me, Mr. Jones?" asked the widow. "It's worth a good deal more than the face of the mortgage."

"You couldn't get a dollar more, in my opinion," said the landlord. "As to takin' you for a tenant, I haven't any assurance that you could pay the rent."

"What rent do you want for it, Mr. Jones?"

"Five dollars a month."

"Five dollars a month, when you say it's only worth two hundred dollars!"

"I'm goin' to fix it up a little," said Mr. Jones, rather nonplussed.

"I think, Mr. Jones, we won't move," said Robert.

"Won't move?" ejaculated the landlord, getting red in the face. "You've got to move."

"Who says so?"

"I say so, you young whelp!"

"No hard names, if you please, Mr. Jones. The fact is, my aunt doesn't fancy going to the poorhouse. To be sure, if she could have your society there it might make a difference."

"You'll repent this impudence, Bob Coverdale!"

"How am I impudent?"

"To talk of my being in the poorhouse!"

"You spoke of Aunt Jane going to the poorhouse."

"That's a different matter."

"At any rate, she won't go!" said Robert decidedly.

"Won't? We'll see about that. How are you going to help it?"

"By paying the mortgage," answered Robert quietly.

"You can't do it," said Mr. Jones, his jaw drooping.

"You are mistaken, Mr. Jones. If you'll write a receipt, I am ready to pay it now—principal and interest."

Robert drew out a roll of bills from the pocket of his ragged vest and began to count them.

"Where did you get this money?" ejaculated the landlord.

"I must decline telling you, Mr. Jones. It's good money, as you can see. I think you'll have to tell Frank Shelton he can't have the house unless he wants to hire of my aunt."

Nahum Jones hated to take the money that was offered him, but there was no loophole to escape. The good bargain was slipping from his grasp. The triumphant look faded from his face, and he looked exceedingly ill at ease.

"I'll come up with you for this, Bob Coverdale!" he muttered angrily.

"For what? Paying you money, Mr. Jones?"

"You know what I mean."

"Yes, I do know what you mean," returned the boy gravely. "This money is in payment for liquor furnished to my poor uncle—liquor which broke up the happiness of his home and finally led to his death. You laid a plot to deprive my aunt, whom you had so much injured, of her home, but you have been defeated. We don't care to have anything more to do with you."

There is no need of recording the landlord's ill-natured answer. He was angry and humiliated, and, when he got home, snapped up Mrs. Jones when she began to make inquiries about the new property. He felt the worse because he had been defeated by a boy.

CHAPTER XXXIV

HOW IT ENDED

"Robert," said Gilbert Huet later in the day, "next week Julian and I go to Boston, where we shall try to make a home for ourselves."

Robert looked sober.

"I shall feel very lonely without you," he said.

"You are to go, too, Robert," said Julian quickly.

"If you will. Julian wants your society, and so do I."

Robert's face flushed with eager delight.

"But my aunt?" he said.

"I have been speaking to your aunt. In fact, I invited her to accompany us, but she says she is used to Cook's Harbor and cannot leave it."

"I don't like to leave her alone."

"Then I'll tell you what you can do. I understand that young Frank Shelton is seeking for a home where he can take his promised wife. I advise you to enlarge the cottage, putting on another story and perhaps an L also. This will give you plenty of room for your aunt and the young couple, who will be company for her."

"Yes," said Mrs. Trafton, "I always liked Frank Shelton and his wife that is to be. The arrangement will be very agreeable to me."

"But," objected Robert, "how can I build an addition to the house? I have no money."

"I beg your pardon," said Mr. Huet, smiling, "but I don't think a young gentleman worth ten thousand dollars can truthfully say he has no money. I hope, Robert, you are not growing mean."

"Ten thousand dollars!" ejaculated Robert, his eyes wide open with amazement.

"Certainly."

"I don't understand you, Mr. Huet."

"Then perhaps you will understand this."

Mr. Huet handed Robert a slip of paper, which proved to be a check on the Merchants' Bank, of Boston, for the sum of ten thousand dollars, payable to Robert Coverdale or order. It was signed by Gilbert Huet.

"You see, you are rich, Robert," said Julian, smiling with joy at his friend's good fortune.

"Oh, Mr. Huet, I don't deserve this," said Robert, his heart full.

"You must let me judge of that, my dear boy. Say no more or you will be depreciating Julian's value. You have restored him to me, and I consider him worth much more than ten thousand dollars."

Of course, Robert joyfully accepted the munificent gift so cordially offered. By Mr. Huet's advice, he invested the money in good dividend-paying securities and monthly sent his aunt twenty-five dollars, which, with the rent, made her quite easy in her circumstances.

The additions were made to the cottage, and Frank Shelton and his wife were glad to hire the house, thus providing Mrs. Trafton with society as well as adding to her income.

As for Robert, henceforth he shared in all the educational advantages which Julian enjoyed.

Mr. Huet took a house, engaged an excellent housekeeper and at length enjoyed a home.

One letter he wrote to Charles Waldo—a scathing letter denouncing him for his infamous conduct and threatening severe punishment if he ever again conspired against his happiness. Mr. Waldo did not answer the letter for very shame. What excuse or apology could he possibly offer?

Three years later Robert and Julian made a vacation journey westward.

"I should like to call on my old friend Nathan Badger," said Julian.

"So should I," said Robert. "I want to see how he looks."

The Badgers could not at first be convinced that the elegant young gentleman, introduced as Julian Huet, was no other than the bound boy, Bill Benton; but he recalled so many incidents of his past life that they credited it at last.

"You were always a favorite of mine, Bill—I mean Mr. Julian!" said the farmer, who had a wonderful respect for wealth.

"And of mine!" chimed in Mrs. Badger. "And I'm sure my Andrew Jackson loved you like a brother."

Andrew Jackson, a gawky youth, no more prepossessing than his boyhood promised, winked hard and looked enviously at Julian.

When the latter drew from his pocket a silver watch and chain and asked Andrew to accept it for old acquaintance sake he was quite overcome and said he liked Julian "better than any feller he knew!"

"Then you forgive me for hitting you with a hoe, Andrew?" said Julian smilingly.

"I don't care for that," said Andrew Jackson stoutly, "and I guess you more'n got even with us that time you stayed with Dick Schmidt and father tried to thrash a tramp—thinking it was you—and got thrashed himself!"

Then Andrew Jackson fixed an admiring glance on the watch he had coveted so long.

"Boys will be boys!" said Mr. Badger with a fatherly smile. "Andrew Jackson don't have no ill feelings."

It was the way of the world. Julian was rich now and had plenty of friends. But he had one true friend whom money could not buy, and this was Robert Coverdale, the young fisherman of Coolers Harbor, prosperous henceforth and happy, as he well deserved to be.

THE END

Printed in Great Britain
by Amazon